Chris Morris is an independent podcast producer. When not  teaches drum kit and percussion at Drum Academy, which he has been running since 2011 and works in a high school as a pupil support assistant.

Chris has been writing for several years but decided in 2020 to finally share some of his writing with the world. He published *Which Way is North?* in November of that year, a book of mixed genre short stories which is available in paperback, Kindle and audiobook formats. He followed this up with *Dreams of a Damselfly*, a novel originally written several years prior which he revisited and re-worked for release in May 2021.

Chris writes and produces a podcast called *Short Stories by Chris Morris*, which can be found wherever you get podcasts. *Joy's Lament* was originally imagined as a short story, then an idea for a podcast Christmas special, until Chris decided it would work best as a short book.

Chris lives in Dundee, Scotland, with his young daughter, Mirryn, who also enjoys listening to, and telling stories.

www.chrisamorris.com

Also by Chris Morris:

Dreams of a Damselfly

An English teacher in Edinburgh is diagnosed with a brain tumour. Trying to keep spirits alive and look out for a bullied boy in her fourth-year class, she decides to follow her dreams rather than allow grief to overcome.

"With a wonderful blend of humor, sadness, adversity and serendipity, this book captures life lessons about how to rise above fear. I highly recommend this book as a heartwarming tear-jerker that delivers eloquent messages of death, survival, love, fear and dignity."
- **Gail Kaufman,** *Indie Book Reviews*

Which Way is North?
15 Mixed Genre Short Stories

A young man whose darkest hour transforms into a superpower that just might help save the world. A mature student who goes back to school to retake his exams. A vampire and a werewolf trying to get along with the locals in a town they have just moved into...

"Each story stands alone, and they are from a variety of genres. Several ended in a way that left me wanting more. The author writes from a place of personal depth and suffering, but overall the book maintains a hopeful tone. His love for his daughter and the tender aspects of his own journey are evident. I would recommend this book!"
- **Laura Miller,** *The Library Laura Podcast*

Available in Kindle, paperback and audiobook formats on Amazon now.

CHRIS MORRIS

-

JOY'S LAMENT

Joy's Lament

Copyright 2021 Chris Morris

First published in 2021 by Chris Morris

Illustrated by MVMET – mvmetmind@gmail.com

Book cover design by bitikcreative

ISBN: 9798463112217

This novella is a work of fiction. Names and characters are the product of the author's imagination and any resemblance to actual persons, living or dead, is entirely coincidental.

All rights reserved. No part of this publication may be reproduced, stored in a retrieval system, or transmitted in any form by any means, electronic, mechanical, photocopying, recording or otherwise, without the prior permission of the copyright owner.

www.chrisamorris.com

'It is required of every man that the spirit within him should walk abroad among his fellow-men, and travel far and wide; and if that spirit goes not forth in life, it is condemned to do so after death. It is doomed to wander through the world – oh, woe is me! – and witness what it cannot share, but might have shared on earth, and turned to happiness.'
- Charles Dickens, *A Christmas Carol*

1
A Spacewoman Came Travelling

Hope.

It was the last thought of the spacewoman as her craft spun out of control and plunged downwards, taking Joy with it.

Below was the source. The root of the problem that had seemingly taken hold of all the universe. The anchor tied to the feet of jubilation as it tried fruitlessly to crawl uphill but was instead dragged inexorably backwards towards the pit of gloom.

But perhaps, just *perhaps* this was the one place the problem could be resolved. And even as she spiralled closer to the surface, the spacewoman couldn't help but cling to that one thing that kept her going, the inspiration for being here and trying against all odds to overthrow whatever great power had its lethal grip tightly clenched around the very throat of all things gleeful.

Hope...

***

The engine was dead: the only sound breaking the enveloping silence was the light flutter of snowflakes as they hit the warm spacecraft, solemnly joining it in its demise. Yes, there was no doubt whatever about it; the condition of the ship was one of two major things that Joy noticed upon waking up. The other being that she had made it. She had arrived.

Outside of the cracked window, Joy observed a frozen planet. The ship had crash-landed awkwardly, with the rear end plunged into several feet of snow, and she had awoken at first to find herself staring upwards, straight into a sun. Instinctively, she had squinted before realising that this planet's sun was much further away than the one she was used to seeing from her own home planet, and besides this, it was veiled behind a thick cluster of clouds, from which the snow fell with grief, like a mourner at a funeral throwing white flower petals before a coffin.

When she looked below this, Joy saw a cold and barren landscape, rolling white hills surrounding patches of forest filled with leafless trees too frozen to sway in the frigid wind that sent the snowflakes crashing quietly to the ground. She let out a few quick gasps of air and watched as it escaped her and joined the smoke soundlessly rise from somewhere on board.

The radio.

Reaching towards the console, Joy found the small, rectangular radio and glanced at the screen. Seventy-eight per cent charged. No signal. Could be worse. She unbuckled herself from the driver's seat and carefully slid out of it, wincing in sudden pain from her ribs and right arm. Glancing outside once more, she felt glad that she'd thrown on her winter coat and gloves, but wondered if it would be enough; this planet looked cold beyond anything she'd experienced back home. Placing the radio in her pocket and walking behind the chair, she fumbled and found the handle to the door, then pulled it before stepping cautiously outside.

The freezing air hit her like an icy thump to the chest. She sharply drew in a breath followed by several gasps of cold, shaking exhales. Climbing down the steps of the ship, her feet eventually found the snow and sank into it. She clumsily flopped forwards as she disappeared almost waist-deep into the snow, her hands racing out in front of her and landing in the cold matter. Catching her breath, she scrambled to an upwards position before wading with great effort towards a small hill with a single, lonely tree at the top; an oyster in a vast white sea of desolation.

Reaching the foot of the hill, Joy clutched on to the roots of the tree and pulled herself upwards, out of the deep snow and underneath the leafless branches where she now sat and brushed the lumps of snow from her trousers, shaking with the raw chill as she did. When she was finished, she reached into her pocket and pulled out the radio. Her heart leapt to discover that it had now found a small signal.

'Come on, come on...' she whispered as her gloved fingers pressed the buttons on the device. The screen flashed a single word:

HOPE

Joy raised the radio high above her head and watched with anticipation for the radio's next move. When it came, her heart sank further into coldness than her ship had:

OUT OF RANGE

'Damn!'

Joy felt like throwing the radio away in frustration, but clutched on to it tightly as she leaned against the bark of the tree and looked at her stolen spacecraft as it sent smoke upwards through the snowflakes and disappeared into the cloudy sky. She crossed her arms around her body and clenched tightly. She would have to move. But in which direction? The radio was of no use and she knew nothing of this place. Which way was north? And even if she knew that, how would this help her? Would her *Sense* work in a place like this?

She decided to sit and think. Think about what it was that led her here in the first place. About her search for the cure to this… this epidemic of grief and despair.

She closed her eyes.

***

Joy was born into a universe that had begun to give up on itself. It had been happening for years, but nobody could say precisely how many. For a long time, people had begun to be… sad. It was the only way to describe it. Despair took the place of happiness everywhere, and for the lengthiest of times, nobody spoke of it. Friends wouldn't dare to console one another, family members watched on quietly as their loved ones became dejected and despondent, preferring their own lonely company over spending happy time in others' comforting presence.

By the time anyone began talking about it, it was already too late; people noticed this sudden grip of sadness that was affecting everyone they knew – but they didn't care. Most had become so filled with sorrow that they cared very little about anything any more. People had forgotten the things that used to make them happy. Smiles became so rare that they looked as though they belonged to another world altogether, somewhere that spirits still shined as brightly as the light from the stars, a place of unfathomable contrast to the grim, stark world that they knew.

Children were also rare. Joy belonged to one of the very last generations of people and she had been named bravely by her parents, who had no doubt held on to hope somewhere in their sunken hearts. Joy was the name given to her at birth, and it was long remarked that she might have been the very last thing in the universe to have been named so.

But even so, there were times of happiness in Joy's life; moments that would warm her heart like a close and loving embrace. Though she mostly had to find these herself. She found glee in simple things – the rolling of a ball down a flight of stairs, the taste of fresh berries, the minute but nonetheless ever-present twinkle in the eyes of those she managed a smile for. Most of all, she enjoyed the singing of birds. Joy and her parents lived in the second-largest city in all of Gylfandell, a technical metropolis which, in normal times, would never cease with the hustle and bustle of electric cars, space shuttles, and factories puffing fetid black plumes of smoke into the air. However, when the people had begun to withdraw into their disheartened states of despair, the city grew quiet and the birds came out again. Many areas of the city become overgrown with plants and weeds of all description, and Joy had found it bleakly beautiful; nature had begun to take over, and with it came the birds. Their joyful songs were the cheeriest things in her life, and Joy loved it.

At the age of five, knowing little else about the world and what it had been like before this dimming of all things happy, Joy had no reason to be alarmed when her parents stopped talking. The last thing she could remember hearing from her father was the announcement of news which should have been exciting, but was said with all the cheer of a visit to a graveyard:

'You're going to have a sibling. A little sister. Or a brother. We don't know yet.'

And for the next few months, Joy watched with fascination and the purest of youthful exhilaration as her mum's tummy got bigger and bigger. She would place a hand on it as her mother slept and feel the baby kick, and a tear would form in her eye as she imagined this little person come into her life and share all the goodness that was still around, the beauty that the world still had to offer which they would surely notice if only the adults would *look* for it – open their eyes and just see it in front of them, hear the birdsong and taste the berries. Laugh, play and *live*.

And although she was only small, and didn't understand things the way the grown-ups did, Joy felt a great conviction in her heavy heart that her parents were missing all of this. They were missing the excitement of a new baby on the way, and they knew nothing of the overjoyed anticipation of their firstborn, who dreamed of nothing else but her unborn little brother or sister and the return of her parents' happiness.

Joy could remember nothing of her parents' voices after the birth of her little sister. They had become withdrawn and muted. She remembered being home with her mother one evening, about a year after the child was born. Her mother held the infant as she slept and Joy's heart greatly desired to take her in her own arms, but she dared not ask. It had been gently snowing that evening, and Joy had gone sledging by herself. She'd wondered if her sister might have enjoyed it. Perhaps she was still too little. She watched her sister now as her little belly expanded and then quickly sank. She was so small. So delicate. So in need of love and support. And she had it. Didn't she?

'Mum?' Joy had piped up. Her mother hadn't answered.

'Mum?' She tried again. 'Can I hold her? My little sister? Can I hold... Mum? What's my sister's name?'

And through the many weeks and months of silence meeting that very question, Joy had slowly realised that her parents never had named the child.

When Joy was eight years old and her little sister was three, their parents disappeared. It had been a dull day; the smog which had once filled the city skyline had almost completely vanished some time ago and looking upwards, Joy could often see the sun peak through the grey clouds. But the day her parents left, the sky had been filled with nothing more than a dark canopy. Joy had been rolling a ball towards her sister, who gladly took it and gently rolled it back to her with a faint smile on her face.

She's still okay, Joy had thought then. *Whatever darkness it is that's taken hold of our parents and everyone else in this city hasn't touched her. Not fully. Not yet...*

'I'm going out,' a low voice had called, and Joy had jumped, startled, for she had long been accustomed to silence in the house but for her and her sister. She glanced up from the ball. It was her father. He already had a hand on the front door and was swinging it open when Joy had spoken up.

'Where are you going? Where's Mum?'

Her father didn't look at her. His eyes lulled downwards and he stared at a part of the floor between his two daughters. 'I don't know,' he said, and then he was gone.

When neither of them had returned that evening, Joy had tried to comfort her sister as she wept and called for her parents. At first, nothing could calm her, but eventually the child's cries quietened and Joy knew in her heart that this was not due to the care she had shown her sister, nothing to do with the warm hugs and the assurances that everything would be fine. No, her sister had ceased crying because she had begun to understand. To understand that her parents were gone and that things wouldn't ever be the same again. There was no point in crying, no point in begging for things to change.

It's begun in her now too, Joy had realised with anguish. *There is nobody safe from this dreadful plague.*

Once her sister was fully quiet and began to close her eyes, Joy told her a story, memorised long ago when stories had still meant much to more people. It was the story of Suree, the mouse who lived on the third moon and was visited by a little girl. Joy used to love the story, and when her mother had stopped telling it and seemed to have forgotten all about it, she'd known that she would have to keep it alive and safe somewhere in her heart. Because she couldn't let a thing like that die.

When she'd finished the story, blown out the candle beside her sister's bed and quietly crept towards the door, a little voice stopped her.

'Joy? Are you going to leave me too?'

And with a tear in her eye, Joy had turned to face the darkness that had hidden her little sister and said: 'No. Never.'

Closing the door behind her and wiping at her face, Joy had made a decision.

Hope. That's what I'll call her. I'll name my little sister Hope. Goodness knows we all need it. And I need her most of all.

***

On the frozen planet, Joy was awoken by a loud beeping sound.

The radio!

Her cold fingers fumbled then gripped the device tightly as she read the message on the screen:

HOPE CALLING

I have signal!

She nearly pressed the wrong button in her alarm. Her hands felt stiff from the bitterness, despite being underneath the thickest and warmest gloves that Joy owned. Pressing the correct button now, she awaited the voice of her sister.

'Hello? Hello? Joy? Can you hear me?'

'H-Hope!' Joy stuttered. 'Yes, yes I can hear you!'

'But I can't see you,' Hope said. Joy looked at the screen. In place of her sister's face was nothing but a dark box with **LOW SIGNAL** scrawled across it.

'No,' Joy said. 'There's not enough signal here. I'm too far away…'

'Where are you?' Hope asked. Her voice sounded anxious.

'I'm…' Joy began. She didn't know what to say. How could she describe it? How could she even begin to explain to her sister? 'You know how I said I think I found the source?'

'Yeah…' Hope's anxiety was slowly becoming alarm.

'Well, I came to find it,' Joy said.

There was a moment's silence before Hope spoke into her radio again. 'What do you mean? You said the source was on another… on another planet. Nobody would take you to another planet.'

'No,' Joy agreed. 'They wouldn't.'

'So how...' Hope began. 'Joy, you need to tell me what's going on!'

Full-out panic now. Joy's heart broke to hear her sister sound so desperately flustered.

'Listen,' Joy said as calmly as she could, but failing to keep her voice from shaking a little. 'It's going to be okay. I took a ship and I just went. I know I can find the source of all of this, and I can fix it.'

'How do you know that?' Hope questioned, and Joy could hear that she was trying to hide the fact that she was quietly sobbing. 'You don't even know what's making everything go all horrible!'

'I'm pretty clever,' Joy said softly. She smiled as she spoke now, hoping that the smile would perhaps come through in her voice. 'They let me work at the observation department and I'm not even twenty yet, remember? I'll work it out.'

Joy's smile was destroyed when Hope spoke again:

'But you said you'd never leave me.'

She went silent. She turned her head away from the radio in fear that Hope may sense her big sister's total anguish. How did Hope remember this? The night their parents left them flashed through Joy's mind like a deep cut that refused to heal.

She wanted to tell Hope that she *hadn't* left her. That she had come to this planet and that she would fix everything really quickly. And even if she couldn't fix anything she'd hop back on the spacecraft and zip back to Hope by tomorrow afternoon. No damage done.

Except the engine is dead. No chance of repair. You're likely stuck here forever. Better to accept it now. Better to just –

She had never lied to Hope and she wouldn't start now. But she didn't want to destroy her either. So what to say?

'Hope...' Joy began. 'I...'

Beep. Beep. Beep.

The signal was lost.

'No!' Joy cried. 'No, no, no! Come on, *come on!*'

She shook the radio and held it high above her head, pointing towards the direction of the now setting sun. It was no use. The signal was gone for now. Perhaps it would be best to move. But where?

The Sense.

It was the only thing that might help Joy now. Hope had always been fascinated by it.

When did you first realise you had it?

Oh, I suppose I've always known, in a way.

What does it feel like?

Nothing, really. You just sort of feel like going in a certain direction and you... just go.

And it always leads you to a memory?

No, not always. Sometimes you've no idea why you've been led to a certain place.

Did Mum and Dad know you had the Sense?

No. They had already gone by the time I fully knew.

The Sense. They said that one in a thousand people on Joy's home planet had it. It was a peculiar thing. Something that, up until now, science had no explanation for. Those with the Sense often felt a pull. They felt drawn to a place of apparent importance to them. Joy often found that she would lose her keys and yet know exactly where to look for them. Once, when Hope was six years old she had wandered off in the middle of a busy Gylfandell, and Joy had known exactly where she'd find her – three streets down in front of an abandoned building that used to be a bakers. She'd always known where to be, and where to find things. It was part of the reason she'd found herself here now, on this frozen planet in search of the very thing that had caused so much despair in the universe.

And with the Sense came that ever more strange ability. The one Joy had to concentrate a little harder on, but provided astonishing results. Joy was able to experience other people's memories. Live and experience them as though they were her own. Mostly this would happen when the person was there, standing in front of Joy. But sometimes she could experience the memories of those who had simply been around a certain place. Joy thought that the memories she saw in this way were some of the most powerful. Left behind and stuck somewhere, refusing to leave like a heavy rock at the bottom of a still pond.

But could she use her Sense here, on this frozen planet? It was certainly worth a try.

Joy pocketed the radio and closed her eyes. She thought about why she was here. She thought about her little sister, Hope in name and all else. She would be happy again. The darkness would do no further damage to her. Her spirits would be lifted and happiness would ring out across the universe once more. If only she knew what was stopping it now. If only she knew where to find that cause of it all...

And there it was. A slight pull to her left.

Across that deep snow and up the hill?

Yes. The Sense almost spoke to her – whispered its advice secretively, as though trying to conceal the information from unfriendly ears. She looked in the direction it was telling her to go and she saw something – movement in amongst the gentle flutter of the falling snow.

A bird. The first sign of life.

It was very small. Brown with a red breast and a yellow beak. It flapped its little wings animatedly and sailed straight towards Joy, who instinctively held out her hand to the creature. With a small tweet, the bird happily flew straight to Joy's outstretched hand and sat there to look up at her, turning its heard to and fro.

Joy couldn't help but smile. 'Why, hello there.'

The bird twittered a little more before moving its head and pointing its beak towards the very place that Joy had felt the pull.

'You want me to go that way too, eh?' Joy said. 'Well alright, but I'm holding you responsible if it's the wrong way.'

The bird made no sound, but tilted its head to the side as if in protest.

'I'm just kidding,' Joy chuckled. 'Are you coming with me then?'

Joy couldn't help but marvel as the bird appeared to understand what she had said; it flew from her hand and towards the snowy hill where it began circling, seemingly waiting for Joy to follow.

'I'm coming, I'm coming,' Joy said, and she followed the bird through the deep snow and up the hill. It was a laborious task; the snow here was once again waist-deep, thinning out as she climbed higher but becoming more slippery here. Joy had to throw her arms out in front of her on more than one occasion to stop herself from plummeting face-first into the snow.

The bird had now perched itself on the bare branch of another tree at the top of the hill, and now watched with interest as Joy trudged through the snow and made her way to the top.

When she'd reached the summit, Joy's breath was taken away.

A village. A little village made up of several small, wooden houses with triangular sloped roofs. Many of them had been overcome by the snow and

buried underneath, their chimneys poking out from below like a submarine's periscope. It looked completely abandoned, and Joy thought that it must have been this way for some time; great clumps of snow had now invaded parts of the village that must have been paths long ago. Not one of the houses emitted a light of any sort, and several unlit lanterns hung frozen all around. And much further away from the last house, perhaps a mile or so, a great and solitary mountain stood, watching over the village like a broad sentry.

'Wow,' Joy breathed to herself. 'Look at this place. But where is everyone?'

She felt a light tap on her right shoulder, and looking around she saw that the bird had now joined her, perched on her shoulder as the pair of them looked down the hill to this quiet, lonely place. A light wind whistling through the branches of the trees and darting around the wooden houses below was all that Joy could hear. She felt as though the wind itself pointed to ancient memories from long ago, too miserable and despairing to consider. And yet she now made her way slowly down the hill and towards the settlement, hoping that perhaps if she found the right memory hidden somewhere within this place, it may lead her to what she was looking for.

The bird flew off again. It fluttered alongside her, occasionally landing softly on top of the snow, much too light to sink into it and leaving delicate footprints beside Joy's wide trudges. Joy shook with the cold as she waded onwards, keeping her eyes fixed on the centre of the village and hoping that there may be a place where she might dry off a little. As she approached what she thought was the first of the wooden houses, Joy spotted one of the small chimneys in front of her and realised that she was already on the roof of one. The bird perched on top of the chimney and chirped at Joy.

'Yeah, yeah, I know,' Joy said in reply. 'I've come a silly way. If I tread softly enough I should be fine, though.'

She carefully walked past the chimney and set one foot gently down at a time, allowing it to sink deep enough into the snow that she was able to lift the other leg and plough forwards. She continued in this way until she moved past the first set of houses buried in snow and into an area of the village that wasn't so covered. Here, walking was easier, and Joy spotted a large building with a wooden cart beside it. Inside the cart were several thick logs, the snow on top of them making them look like some sort of iced cake. Many more wooden logs were gathered in neat piles here and there.

Perhaps an old lumberjack's cabin, Joy thought.

The door to the cabin was raised out of the deepest parts of the snow by a front porch. Joy walked over to it, tried the door and found dishearteningly that it was locked. Peering through the glass panel of the door, she could make out very little through the darkness inside, besides some candles that had been placed by the door.

The bird, who had been sitting happily on the raised wall of the porch, chirped once again and flew off towards another of the houses, circling around it and whistling for Joy's attention.

'That one?' Joy queried. 'If you say so, little one.'

Before she left the cabin, Joy felt a sudden but soft memory come to her. It was not strong or detailed; simply a feeling. A feeling that a happy family had once lived here, but all that lingered now was a mournful shadow of things that might have best been forgotten.

On her way towards the house the bird was circling, Joy observed more about the village. Many old lanterns hung from long ropes that had extended house-to-house through large parts of the place. They were an assortment of faded colours and now hung ice-covered and crestfallen in the emptiness. Many of the houses had painted models of various animals sitting in the snow beside them. Joy spotted what looked to her like deer, rabbits, squirrels and more birds. Beside many of these, a tree had been placed, decorated with coloured wooden balls and wrapped with brilliant pieces of silver and golden materials. At the top of many of these trees sat a silver star. And in the very centre of the village stood the biggest tree of them all, partly sunken but standing tall and grandiose, decorated in much the same way as all of the others.

Perhaps there had been some sort of festival or celebration here, Joy thought. *Must have been a long time ago.*

Reaching the house she'd been walking towards, the bird fluttered down and sat softly on Joy's shoulder as she reached for the door handle, turned it and found that she could swing the door open easily. The sun had almost fully set now, and darkness enveloped the inside of the house. Yet, Joy knew exactly where to look. To the side of the door was a small cabinet and on top of this, a lantern. Reaching down below, Joy pulled open a drawer and found a box of matches. She lit the lantern.

She was thankful for the light, but ever more grateful for the warmth coming from it. She shut the front door behind her, hoping to keep much of the warmth inside, and held the lantern close to her. Looking around, she saw a neat house, but nothing lavish. Mostly everything was made from wood, besides an old-fashioned iron kettle and a stone fireplace.

Fireplace!

Joy immediately made her way to this and saw that there was much fresh wood to be used. Having little experience in making fires herself, she didn't know what to do quite yet, but her Sense once again whispered to her, and a fire was going before too long. Joy found a comfortable chair and pulled it towards the fireplace. The bird, who had been watching Joy curiously from afar, now swooped over to her and sat on her lap beside the glowing fire.

'You like that?' Joy asked. 'I thought you'd be used to this cold.'

Joy removed her gloves before pulling the radio out of her pocket. Her hands were red. She looked at the screen.

SEARCHING FOR SIGNAL...

Give it a few moments, she thought. *It may find something.*

She looked down at the bird on her lap. Its eyes were half-closed and it sat as still as undisturbed water. Its red breast and yellow beak made it look very similar to a type of bird from Joy's home. Her favourite, in fact. Once the birds had started coming back into the city, the red-breasted ones were among those who had sung the merriest and lifted Joy's spirits. She had never known what they were called; asking her parents had proven futile, and she hadn't known where else to look for this information.

'Why did you lead me here, then?' Joy asked the bird. It looked up at her inquisitively, but made no sound. 'Is there something important here? Did you know whoever lived here?'

Joy pondered this as she begun to feel light-headed. She sunk deep into the chair and slowly began to close her eyes. She could feel it coming. It was very strong. There was memory here, yes. Vivid, powerful memory. And it may have been just what Joy was looking for.

She closed her eyes fully and let the memory take her.

~

Light. Bright and wholesome light. It was the first thing these little eyes noticed upon opening. All different shades and colours of it, illuminating the room in excited splendour.

The little one turned his head to look at the big window. Snow was trickling down gently from the sky and it must have been morning now, because everything was bright and beaming. Looking up to the ceiling again, he saw that the funny ornament was still hanging there, beautiful and happy. He liked the animals on it. Especially the bird. Its red tummy was nice and he liked the way it looked to be smiling with its yellow beak. But why had they covered it with those colourful paper circles? Maybe just for fun?

He yawned and then felt something. Something uncomfortable. He wriggled his bum from side to side. It didn't feel nice. Not at all. He needed someone. Mummy or Daddy. Why weren't they coming already? Didn't they *know* he needed them?

He wailed.

That did the trick. Here was Mummy, fussing over him and smiling that wide, happy smile that always calmed him a little.

'Oh, Lothar!' she beamed. 'What's wrong, my son? What's all this noise about?' And then, sniffing the air, she placed one hand to cover her nose and used the other to waft the air in front of her. 'Oh, I see. Let's get you sorted then.'

In no time at all, Lothar's mother had taken away the old cloth, cleaned him up and tied on a fresh, new piece of cloth in the old one's place.

'There,' she said, smiling at the boy. She lowered herself to him and softly kissed him on the nose. 'Merry Christmas, Lothar.'

'Christmas!' a loud, excited voice called from another room. 'It's Christmas! Wake up, Jonas!'

The sound of rushing feet rebounded around the house and shortly after, Lothar's older brother and sister appeared at the doorway, breathless.

'Can I wake Father?' Jonas asked, eagerly.

'If he hasn't awoken already I'll eat the Christmas tree. Go on then, see if he's up!'

The children disappeared at once and from the sounds of it, they launched themselves onto their father's bed, landing on top of him with a hard smack before he grumbled something about breaking the bed frame.

'What are they like, eh?' Lothar's mother grinned at him. 'Silly old Jonas and Annika. Your siblings are mad.'

A rumbling of rushing feet now sounded from the parents' room and Lothar's brother and sister appeared shortly afterwards once more.

'Father says we can go downstairs!' Annika beamed. 'Can we, Mother? Oh, please say we can!'

'Of course you can,' their mother smiled. 'Your father has already said as much. But don't open anything until we're all there.'

Saying nothing more, the children rushed away and baby Lothar could hear them exclaim in delight as they discovered whatever it was that was down there.

Appearing at the door now was Lothar's father, a large, bearded man whose smile could still be observed no matter how much hair obscured it.

'How's the little one, Malin?' he asked. 'Is he terribly elevated for his first Christmas?'

'Well, he certainly got everyone up early,' Malin smiled. 'Perhaps he does sense the joy in the air.'

Lothar's father walked into the room now and kneeling down beside Malin, kissed her softly on the mouth. 'Merry Christmas, my love.'

'Merry Christmas, Sander.'

'Mother! Father! Are you coming down yet!?'

Malin and Sander smiled at one another. It made Lothar feel happy. He was so used to seeing them like this; his parents with happy smiles spread widely across their faces. Often, he could feel the warmth exude from them and wrap itself lovingly around him like a protective and tender blanket. It made his heart sing and he thought that if things would be like this forever, he'd be content and glowingly satisfied for all time.

'Yes, yes!' Sander called. 'We're coming!'

Malin lifted Lothar and held him close to her breast. Together with Sander, they walked down the stairs to meet their older children.

***

Underneath the Christmas tree, Sander and Malin had left several gifts beautifully wrapped in paper of many different colours and carefully decorated with elegant bows. Sander had joked that he hadn't seen the point in making the gifts look so lovely; the children would tear them open in mere seconds. Malin had more faith in her children; she had assured Sander that the little ones held much more self-restraint than he had presumed, and besides, they all knew how special a day Christmas was for each member of the family. Both older children would be as excited as anyone else to watch others open their gifts.

And Malin was right. When the parents had come down the stairs they patiently awaited while their father tried without success to start the fire. They waited further while little Lothar was handed over to Jonas so that their mother could take over fire duty, and giggled to see their father's reddened face when the fire was started in half the time that he had been struggling with it.

While all of this was going on, Lothar's little eyes were fixed upon the strange but beautiful tree that his parents had put in the house. There were many trees in and around the village, but they were always outside. It was a strange sight to see this one hauled indoors and then decorated with several bright and colourful things. He had watched with interest some time ago as his brother and sister painted wooden balls, and with their father's help cut a little hole into them so that little pieces of string could be threaded through them. Here they hung on the branches of the tree now, some painted with patterns, others with pictures of deer or birds or snowflakes. Ribbons that his mother had carefully knotted had been placed alongside these, and at the very top stood a golden star. They had given this to Lothar and held him high up to the top of the tree, but he hadn't placed it there; he had clutched on to it and stared at it in wonder. It was a thing so beautiful that he hadn't wanted to let it go.

The family took turns in opening their gifts. Annika was first. She'd marvelled at the main gift: a great wooden castle alongside small wooden figures of a king and queen, prince and princess, and even a large red dragon and a brave, armoured knight to battle it.

Jonas was hugely pleased with his marble maze; a large wooden board with many ledges, through which a small marble was guided by tilting to and fro. He had always adored games such as these, and it became an obsession to try to beat his record time with each new attempt.

Malin's beautiful silver necklace and Sander's new large axe were also greatly appreciated. Sander remarked humorously that he might make Elias jealous, for the old lumberjack across the path had been thwacking away with an old, blunting axe for nearly an entire year now.

For little Lothar, his mother had gifted him a thing which had instantly caught his attention and admiration, and he had spent the rest of the day cradling it carefully: indeed, remarkably carefully for such a young baby. The moment his father had helped him tear off the lemon-yellow paper, Lothar had become enamoured with the little stuffed toy bird. It was his favourite of the real-life birds that he would occasionally see flutter past outside; the little one with the red belly and the yellow beak. He longed to reach out and touch one of them, just to see what the little things felt like. Holding this one now and feeling how soft it was filled Lothar with a sort of joy and serenity that was difficult to understand.

'He loves his bobin!' Annika remarked, brightly.

'Yes,' Sander agreed. 'I've never seen him so focused on something before. Besides that old star for the tree, perhaps.'

More gifts were opened, and some smaller toys were offered to Lothar, who kept his attention focused on his bird instead of anything else. This was met with much laughter, and Malin had in jest said that perhaps they needn't have bothered finding any other gifts for the baby. The older children enjoyed opening more toys and a few sweet treats – some that their father had baked himself and others that their mother had procured from the famous bakers in Lyran, a town some thirty miles to the east.

The fireplace emitted a warm light that lit the little house in a calm but joyous glow; the snowfall had by this point become much heavier, and the sky was darkened with heavy grey clouds. This made for a magnificent view outside the window, for the village was shrouded in a light darkness but lit up handsomely by the multicoloured lanterns that hung all over. Some were even attached to the great Christmas tree not far from the house, and these cast wonderful bright and colourful shadows in the snow and on many of the houses.

'Isn't it spectacular!' Sander exclaimed, looking out. 'Never have I seen such a sight on any Christmas in all my years!'

Jonas had joined him on his father's knee, his eyes widened broadly as he gazed out upon the marvel of his home village. Malin joined them at their side carrying Lothar, and Annika squeezed in between her father and her mother, who placed her free arm around her shoulders.

They saw many other villagers pass by, merrily wishing each other a happy Christmas, several of them going to the doors of their neighbours with gifts.

'We should make our rounds soon too,' Malin said. 'Otherwise the rest of the village may think we've abandoned the old tradition!'

'It will have to wait just a moment,' Sander said with a chuckle. 'It seems the first of our visitors have arrived.'

Sure enough, they welcomed Albin and Tuva into their home, who had brought gifts of wine for

Sander and Malin, chocolates for Jonas and Annika, and some pyjamas for Lothar which Tuva had weaved herself.

'My, my!' Albin had exclaimed upon seeing Lothar. 'What do you have there? A nice little bobin! How lovely!'

The couple stayed long enough to exchange gifts, engage in some pleasant chatter, and then they were off, they said, to visit old Helena, who had become slower in her older years and wasn't much up to trekking around the other houses of the village.

'Yes, I imagine she may get a visit from every person in the village today,' Malin said. 'We plan to go later too.'

Sander had looked out a list he had compiled with Malin's help a few days earlier. He crossed off the names of Albin and Tuva and began discussing the best route through the village when there was another knock at the door.

'I'll get it!' Jonas called.

And barely a minute after they had said goodbye to their previous guests, in came five more – Gunnar, his wife Clara, and their three children, who ran around the house and played so merrily with Jonas and Annika that whatever cheer had already been present in the house was multiplied tenfold. Much fuss was made over baby Lothar, who still held on wondrously to his bird.

The morning passed quickly in this way, almost automatically – guests would leave and more would arrive, Sander scribbled furiously on his list as he crossed off more names and made adjustments to the route they would take through the village when they got the chance to leave. Gifts were exchanged and much laughter and cheer was invited time and again into the house. Lothar, being so young and not yet at the stage to understand any of this fully, was not immune to the feeling of happiness, gratitude and warmth touching his own heart.

When they finally had a large enough break in receiving guests, Sander and Malin instructed the older children to fetch their coats, hats, gloves, scarves and boots. Sander held on to Lothar while Malin checked their many bags against the list. The toys for Fredrik and Susanne's children, the warm scarves for their parents, the whisky for Odin, the rum for Eva, the new axe for the lumberjack (oh, wait until they saw his face!), the freshly baked scones for Ingrid. Yes, yes, everything seemed to be here; with some assistance from young Annika and Jonas they may just be able to make it around the village in one go. When they were ready to leave, they swung the front door widely open and entered a joyful scene indeed.

The snow glided down in brilliant flurries, but the paths were smartly cleared by many shovels and much sea salt. The vast cheer and enthusiasm in the air was infectious enough that it might have lifted the spirits of the most downcast of people, of which there were none to find. Lothar watched on through eyes which had been partly and mistakenly covered by a thick woollen hat that was just a little too big for him. Many smiling faces passed and all of them stopped at least for a moment to wish the family a merry Christmas, and to further congratulate them on the birth of their third child, born only two months before. Sometimes they would pass those whom they had yet to visit and exchanged gifts there and then on the path. Sander worked hard at remembering these names for his list, crossing them off at the next home they visited with the generous loan of a quill.

As they neared the western side of the village, Annika and Jonas had excitedly pleaded with their parents to allow them just one or two goes at sliding down the great hill that was popular with all of the children in the settlement.

'But we didn't bring your sledges!' Malin protested.

'It's okay!' a smiling child trudged up to family, puffing. 'There are plenty of spares!'

'Alright,' Sander said. 'You can have three goes.'

'Thank you, Father!' Jonas beamed, and he ran off with his sister and the other child.

Sander and Malin watched with pleasure as their older children joined in with dozens of others in sliding down the hill. They appeared to be racing each other, zipping down the hill on the borrowed wooden sledges head first and colliding with a great mound of snow which had been gathered at the bottom.

'Look, Lothar!' Sander said to the baby. 'Look how brave and wild your brother and sister are!'

But Lothar only glanced up for a few moments before returning his gaze to the brown and red bobin he still clutched through his warm, gloved hands.

***

When all gifts with their fellow villagers had been exchanged, and Annika and Jonas had finally been pulled away from a friendly snowball fight, the family found that they were just in time for the annual carol-singing around the great bonfire that had been erected near the village Christmas tree. Most folk in the village would attend, and this year was no different. Several villagers went around to give mugs of hot tea or sweetened chocolate drinks, and all sang a selection of Christmas songs as they enjoyed the warmth from the fire. At the end of it, many more merry Christmases were exchanged, and Lothar's family returned home.

Malin set another fire at once. The older children played with their new toys, and welcomed the opportunity to mind their baby brother while he slept, presumably exhausted from the day's excitement. He had awoken now, and made no sound as he watched his smiling siblings play together in the warm light from the fireplace.

Lothar's siblings were later called to set the table and he soon joined them in a special high-seated chair that Sander had built himself many months previously. He was full from his mother's milk, which he'd taken just after his nap, and watched on with interest as the rest of the family enjoyed a feast of a meal that emitted a pleasant aroma Lothar enjoyed.

He watched as Annika and Jonas pulled a cracker together, and out poured tissue paper of all colours. Jonas held the larger end and dug his hand through it until he found a chocolate and a small piece of paper. Unfolding it he read aloud:

Christmas is joyous, Christmas is fun,
With chocolates, fruit and buns,
But watch out for putting too much in your belly,
For tomorrow might come something awful and smelly.

The children roared with laughter at this, but Malin had given Sander a look of playful scorn.

'Sander! It's supposed to be *nice* poems in the crackers! Besides, the rhythm was all off in yours.'

'Well, let's see how much better you did!' Sander returned, and the children pulled the other cracker. Jonas once again held the bigger part, but handed this over to his sister who read aloud the next unfolded piece of paper:

Never shall we forget today,
The joy, the laughter, the gifts and play,
Baby's first Christmas and all good cheer,
Spent with those we adore and hold dear,
But lest we forget what holds most true,
Should ever we feel sorrow and know not what to do,
We need not spend forever looking around,
This family brings comfort and happiness abound.

'That's a really nice poem, mother,' Jonas said.

'Thank you, my love,' Malin beamed. She turned to her husband for his reaction, but Sander had stood up to turn his face away from her.

***

Tears. It was all Lothar could manage now. So tired. So spent. He was ready for his mother and father to change him and put him to bed where he longed to close his eyes and dream of bobins.

'Come, Lothar, my little one.'

Sander took the boy in his arms and the rest of the family followed him up the stairs of their house. After a quick change into some fresh pyjamas, Lothar was placed gently into his cot and his mother sang a Christmas carol. Holding onto his soft bird, he watched the happy faces of his family fade until he dozed off into a comfortable slumber.

2
God Rest Ye Merry, Gentlefolk

'Fortune,' Joy said. 'I'll call you Fortune.'

She had just opened her eyes. The bird – the *bobin* as it seemed to be known as in this world – was now sitting lazily on her lap and might have been drifting off when Joy stirred it. It looked up at her now with quizzical eyes, leaning its small head to the side questioningly.

'I was fortunate enough to meet you,' Joy said. 'It seems you led me to a place of importance, somehow. That was a strong memory.'

Fortune made no response. The bird nestled its beak into the feathers on its back and closed its eyes.

Looks like I did disturb you after all, Joy thought. *Sorry, little one.*

'You're a girl too, aren't you? Like me.'

Fortune made no further response. She kept her eyes closed and her beak settled into her warm feathers.

Joy looked around her. She was in no doubt that this house was the very same from the memory she had just experienced; this was how Joy's Sense usually worked, after all. Memories were left behind at the place their owners remembered them. Not wanting to disturb Fortune, she leaned forwards in the chair very slightly to look out of the window. She couldn't see much more than the very edges of some of the homes that surrounded the one she was in, but she could see the huge tree from here, frozen and still in the dark cold. How bleak it now was. How beautiful it used to be.

If this really was the place responsible for the loss of joy around the universe, if this was where it had all started, then the people in that memory should have been miserable. They should have been devoid of all cheer. The memory must have been an old one. A very old one. But what happiness there was! Joy had never seen anything like it back home. How could the spread of misery have come from a place so filled with radiant glee? What happened here? And where was everyone now?

The fire was dying, but still warm. Filled with the affection of the memory she had experienced and satisfied by the glow from the fire, Joy closed her eyes again and drifted off.

***

She was awoken by a crash.

Fortune fluttered swiftly from Joy's lap and disappeared into the darkness of the house; the fire had gone out, leaving nothing but a few glowing embers that were now fading into nothing.

'Fortune!' Joy cried. She looked around but could make nothing out in the shadows.

Outside, she heard rushing footsteps. Moving too quickly to be anything human. The sound moved quickly from one side of the house to the other, and became fainter as whatever was out there scuttled away.

A deer, perhaps? She'd seen pictures of them; this planet had them too, or creatures very like them. But no, it sounded too large to be a deer. But what if they were just bigger than the ones back home?

No. Something deep within Joy told her that whatever she had heard was nothing friendly. Images of nightmarish creatures came into her mind, and thinking of these in the darkness did nothing for her nerve. Scrambling for a moment in the darkness, she found the lantern and re-lit it.

'Fortune? Fortune, where are you?'

She found the bobin perched on top of what looked like an empty bookcase. She was breathing rapidly, her chest moving in and out in quick bursts as her eyes fixed widely on the window behind Joy.

'It's okay,' Joy said, calmly. 'Whatever that was is gone now. Come on, let's get out of here. Maybe you can show me where to go next?'

Fortune remained still for a moment longer, but her eyes finally moved from the window to Joy, and then she glided down to perch once more on her shoulder.

'That's it,' Joy smiled. 'Nothing's going to hurt you while I'm here. I promise.'

Deciding that Fortune may still be a little too shaken to guide her anywhere for the time being, Joy thought it might be a good idea to have a look around the house. Maybe she would find a clue as to why this place was so important. Why had she observed that memory though the eyes of a little baby named Lothar? What had happened to him and his family? She feared that the answers to these questions, while likely helpful to her, may not be particularly happy.

She lit the fireplace again and looked around her. This part of the house was nothing more than a wide area which contained several chairs, a table, the fireplace and a kitchen area. A large, dusty rug had been laid out on the floor, and Joy recognised the area where the tree had been in the memory.

'This is where little Jonas and Annika opened their gifts,' Joy said.

It was a thing called *Christmas*. Some sort of festival or celebration that was completely alien to Joy. It had seemed something which brought great happiness and excitement to the people of the village. Especially the children. But there were no toys here now. What happened to Annika's castle? Jonas' games? They had disappeared. Just like the people. Just like happiness.

A set of wooden stairs led to a mezzanine and doors that Joy knew led to bedrooms. Perhaps something there would help her. She climbed the stairs slowly, holding the lantern out in front of her. It gradually got darker as she moved away from the fireplace. The first door must have been the one she had seen Lothar wake up inside. She gently swung this door open and peered inside.

It was very different to how she had seen it before. No baby's cot, but a normal-sized bed with a small cabinet next to it. A wardrobe and a chair were the only other items in here. Joy almost decided it wasn't worth investigating and made to leave before Fortune glided off her shoulder and zipped over to the bedside cabinet.

'Fortune, there's nothing in here,' Joy said. But Fortune began chirping and jumping up and down. Joy took a step further into the room and saw that there was a piece of paper underneath Fortune's feet.

'Oh!' Joy started. How hadn't she seen it?

She walked over to Fortune and the bobin once again flew to her and perched on her shoulder. Joy picked up the paper and, glancing at it, suddenly felt an overwhelming sense of sadness.

She couldn't say exactly what was sad about it. It should have been a happy thing to see, but a sea of despair and hopelessness was somehow attached to it. It was a child's drawing. No colour, just a black and white image of a man and a little girl sitting side by side. Both of them were smiling; not just through their U-shaped mouths but also through their beady, black eyes which, even though they were nothing more than two black circles, somehow held a childish sort of shine. In the air surrounding the two figures, several lovehearts floated.

Joy put a hand to her mouth, and then moved it to wipe the tear from her eye. Who were these people? Just a single adult and a child – remarkably different to what Joy had seen in this place before. What happened to the big family?

It was entirely possible, Joy thought, that the man depicted in this image may have been Jonas as a man, perhaps even Lothar; the old memory she'd witnessed must have taken place some time ago. Far enough into the past that enough time might have come and gone for all of the children to have become grown adults. But then, why would they still reside in their parents' old house? And who was this little girl? Where was she now?

She shuddered as some grim thoughts roughly pushed their way into her mind.

'Come on, Fortune,' Joy said. 'Let's see if we can find any more clues.'

She gently placed the picture down onto the bed and turned to leave. There were another three doors to open. There was nothing much among the clutter of the first or second. Old boxes filled with trinkets that seemed to be of little importance, dusty cobwebs that had long been abandoned by their creators, peculiar objects that vaguely resembled musical instruments from Joy's home planet. But the third room had clearly belonged to the child who had drawn the picture.

In here, Joy found some small toys as dusty as the webs from the previous rooms. They looked as though they hadn't been played with for a long time. It might have suggested to Joy that the home had been vacated for a long time if it weren't for the many pictures that lay strewn all over the room – on the little bed, the floor, the desk and chair to the side. Some were even stuck on to the wall with drawing pins. Most of them were mournful.

She saw some that were of a similar nature to the one found in the father's bedroom – smiling, happy faces, a parent and child holding hands, playing together, cuddling. Some were of the girl playing with other children. These pictures were even drawn with some colour, and Joy was intrigued to know how this was achieved; she had only seen a quill used as something to write with here. Perhaps they used inks of various colours? One drawing that particularly caught Joy's eye was of a group of girls holding hands in a circle. They looked as though they were spinning around and having fun. But to the side of this group of children, and further off in the distance was another little girl who sat lonely, hugging her knees to her chest and looking at the ground in front of her with a sad face. In her eye was a single, blue tear.

The pictures Joy spotted from here were a strange mixture of glee and sorrow. They used less colour now and had become much flatter. Most of them involved the father. The first of these that Joy spotted was a picture of the man sitting by the fireplace while the girl stood behind him and next to one of those green, decorated trees. In every picture that the child had drawn of another person, the mouth was always a clear U shape for a smile, and an upside-down U for a frown. But this drawing of the girl's father was different; the mouth was drawn as a single horizontal line.

And after this picture, Joy had only seen despair. Every face that the girl had drawn wore a frown. None of them had colour.

Fortune flapped away from Joy and landed on the floor beside a colourful and smiling picture of the girl. She did something queer then; she gently touched the tip of her beak to the drawing and nudged it gently, as though trying to get the child's attention. After she'd done this two or three times, she simply sat and looked at the picture with a tilted head.

Joy felt remorse wrap itself around her.

'Come on, Fortune,' she said. 'I can't stay in here. This place is making me feel much too sad.

But the bobin didn't move. She began chirping loudly now, still looking at the girl's picture.

'Fortune, please,' Joy pleaded. 'I'm not leaving you in here but I can't stay.'

The bird continued chirping. To Joy, it sounded mournful, bleak, despairing. Like it was grieving the loss of something special. It tore at Joy's heart like a flame burning harshly through the wick of a candle. Tears now began streaming down her cheeks, flowing out of her like water from a sponge.

'*Fortune!*'

Bang.

They were interrupted by another huge sound, just like the one that had frightened Fortune so much earlier. It stopped her chirping dead and the bird now flew swiftly once again to Joy's shoulder where she trembled.

'What is it?' Joy whispered. 'You *know* what's out there, don't you?'

Fortune made no sound in reply, but sat on Joy's shoulder with wide eyes, tense and rigid except for the rapid breathing and shaking.

I need to find out what it is...

Leaving the child's bedroom behind, Joy rushed down the stairs and to the window by the fireplace. She extinguished the flame of the lantern and peered out. Darkness. Nothing to see, except she now heard those rushing footsteps again. They were coming from her left. Turning her head that way, she spotted something. A large, black shadow among the white of the snow. It was moving quickly – much too quickly for Joy to be able to make out exactly what it was. And in the blink of an eye, it sped past the house and off into the distance, past the great tree and into an area of the village that Joy hadn't explored.

And that's when she knew.

'I'm really sorry,' she said to Fortune. 'But I think I have to follow it.'

***

She'd lit the lantern again. Outside the house it gave off just enough light for her to see the area directly in front of her, and she could make out other objects by squinting and straining her eyes. The bite of the cold out here was painful after her short rest inside the old house of baby Lothar. She had felt much remorse when she had had to extinguish the fire inside the house, not knowing when she may next find somewhere with such warmth.

Beside her, Fortune had regained some composure. Joy had told her that she didn't have to come with her. Speaking to the bird was strange, but she seemed fascinatingly intelligent, and Joy thought that she could understand at least some of what she was saying to her. Nevertheless, it was comforting to have a companion, a friend to talk to. She'd wondered if the bird might well stay put in the house, or at least fly off somewhere much safer (having become very fond of her, Joy had in fact *feared* this), but she stood with her now, as loyal a thing as anyone could wish for.

She trudged onwards.

They soon came to a part of the village that Joy somewhat recognised from Lothar's memory.

'This is where Jonas and Annika went sledging with the other kids in the village,' she mumbled quietly. Fortune softly tweeted in return.

They had indeed arrived at the foot of the large hill. Only, it looked markedly different; gone were the many lines in the snow where the sledges had cut into it as they drifted gleefully downwards. Surely either because of the heavy snowfall or the sad fact that children no longer sledged here. Looking to the bottom of the hill was enough to see that the latter was true. As Joy neared, and the lantern lit the space in front of them more clearly, she could see that a great fence had been erected, and in the middle of this, a gate.

'I think we should take a look, Fortune,' Joy said.

She didn't want to. Even from here she could sense a heavy heartbreak hauntingly escape this place and drift its way towards her like a lost spirit searching for its misplaced cheer.

But then, wasn't it clinging on to her anyway? Yes, it hadn't disappeared since visiting the child's room in Lothar's old house and seeing the despairing pictures. Joy had assumed that getting out of there would have been enough for that feeling of complete overwhelming sadness to fade away. But it seemed it hadn't been. It was still there, clutching on to Joy and refusing to let go.

Has it finally happened? Am I finally becoming the latest victim?

But those thoughts wouldn't do, Joy decided. Not here, not now. There was a great task at hand. It required focus. Joy moved towards the gate.

As she approached, she saw the structure in more detail. The bottom was made of stone and a large iron fence stood above it. The bars of the fence were somewhat bent, some of them nearly touching and others pointing away from, or into whatever lay inside. And here, at the great iron gate, Joy saw that it was locked with a chain.

'Damn,' she muttered. 'How am I supposed to get in?'

She looked around. Maybe she could climb a nearby tree and drop herself inside? Nothing. She held the lantern out in front of her and scanned the fence line. She spotted an area of the fence that was particularly poorly made with a small gap between the bars that she thought she might be able to squeeze through.

As though sensing Joy's plan, Fortune fluttered from her shoulder and landed softly somewhere on the other side of the fence. Joy took a deep breath in and began her attempt to slip through the gap. She put the lantern through first and then stepped a leg over the stone wall and into the snow on the other side. She had to uncomfortably duck her head down a little as she made her way slowly through, but finally made it, and holding the lantern in front of her, let out a short, shaken gasp.

It was a graveyard. No doubt about it. Many tall stones stood here and there, and Joy thought she could make out lettering on some of them, even from where she now stood. At the foot of only three that Joy could see were some flowers. It was impossible to tell how old these were; they were all frozen stiff.

She moved forwards and came to a small wooden sign. Holding the lantern close to it, she read:

In memory of those who fought to keep joy and hope alive

The words haunted Joy. Suddenly, what felt like a thousand thoughts and feelings made themselves known to her, and that sense of despair that had been clasping to her now began to wrap itself around her as though trying to suffocate her. Well, here she was. She had stolen a spacecraft and fled Gylfandell to be here, leaving the very thing she could call Hope behind.

And she realised now that she was weeping. But for what? For the gradual loss of hope? For the people buried in this place? Buried, seemingly fighting some war that she now thought she could put an end to by wandering around and investigating?

And as if in response, the radio sounded.

She fumbled for it. Finding it in her pocket she yanked it out, nearly dropped it, and then instantly answered the call.

'Hope? Hope, is that you?'

'Yeah...' the voice sounded dejected.

'I'm so glad to hear your voice!' Joy said, and she even smiled genuinely.

'Have you found anything yet?' Hope asked, almost disinterestedly.

'No, not really,' Joy replied. 'Except I did find a memory. From a long time ago, I think.'

Silence on the other end of the radio.

'Hope? Are you still there?'

'Yeah, I'm here.'

'Don't you want to hear about the memory?'

There was a pause. And then, 'Yeah.'

With some uneasy hesitance, Joy recounted the memory of baby Lothar as best as she could remember it. The happy family, the wonderful lights, the grandiose décor of the village. As she talked about the exchange of gifts between every soul in the place her own heart began to trepidatiously lift as though she herself had been a part of it, and she was now simply recalling a gleeful time from her own childhood. Her little sister never interrupted once and Joy became immersed and lost in her retelling. She only became fully aware of Hope's silence when she had finished talking. There were a few heavy seconds of still hush before Hope spoke, her voice marginally more bright than before.

'That's lovely.'

Joy wheezed. A sob escaped her.

'Joy? Are you okay?'

This made things even worse. She took a moment to compose herself before speaking again.

'I'm fine. I just... I thought I'd lost you. You sounded so distant.'

'Did I?' Hope asked. 'Sorry. I've just been worried, I think. Your story has cheered me up a little.'

'Good,' Joy said. 'Me too.'

She hadn't told Hope about finding the child's drawings, and even the thought of them now seemed to send a sharp spike through the distant memory of Lothar's first Christmas. She shook it off. She couldn't allow her mind to go back there. She had to focus on Hope. Stay completely focused on Hope.

'So where are you now?' Hope asked.

Joy took a deep breath. 'I'm in some sort of graveyard. One that was built for people who fought in some sort of war.'

'Oh,' Hope replied. The sad tone in her voice suddenly reappeared.

'But this is good,' Joy went on quickly. 'Whatever these people fought against and died for *must* be what I'm looking for. I'm sure of it, Hope. If I can access someone's memory from this place, I might well find out what I can do.'

'Does your Sense work with dead people?' Hope asked.

It was a dreary question, but a good one. Joy had no clear proof that her Sense *did* work with those who had passed away. But then, what about Lothar? Had his memory been so long ago that his time in this world had already passed?

And there, once again, that creeping feeling of hopeless sorrow began wriggling back.

Shake it off. Smile. Force yourself.

'Yeah,' Joy said. 'I'm sure it does.'

And then, as though her sister had become some great invigilator testing Joy on how well she could keep it all together, Hope said, 'Is the spaceship alright?'

No. No it's not alright. It's irreversibly broken and unless this planet has some spaceships of their own and a pilot willing to take me back home (which, going by the level of technology I've seen here so far, is more than incredibly unlikely), I'm stuck here forever. Even if I put an end to this war on happiness I'll be stuck here, and the only time we'll have left to talk to each other will be ruthlessly stopped by the death of the battery in this radio. The observation department won't send anyone on a rescue mission for me, not after I stole one of their ships and wrecked it on an alien planet. Whether I grow old here and die in my sleep or I freeze to death trying to find the cure for sadness, I'm already gone. Gone like Mum and Dad. Gone like –

'Joy?'

Hope's voice interrupted. It sounded crackly.
'J y?'
Oh no!
She looked at the screen on the radio. The signal was failing.
'Hope? Hope! Can you still hear me? Hope!'
Beep. Beep. Beep.

***

Tears. Cold, hard tears streaming down the face of Joy. Tears like those wept by baby Lothar long ago.

She pounded her fists into the snow. She looked up to the dark sky and screamed at the falling snowflakes, many of which fled in all directions, away from the wrath of the only human seen for many a day.

She collapsed in a heap into the icy cold ground.

And then she heard something that sounded disturbingly like laughter. A low, evil kind of laughter.

She didn't need her Sense or the fact that Fortune fled into the flurry to know that whoever, *whatever* had laughed was the thing that had darted past the house of Lothar and sped into the darkness.

It was watching from the shadows.

***

Her Sense guided her now. Pulled her, tugged at her sleeve like a child eager to show his mother something special. But she knew that whatever it was she was about to find would not be happy.

She trekked tirelessly through the snow and past many great stones. She had relit the lantern, which had accidentally been extinguished when Joy had despairingly thrown herself to the ground a moment before. She could make out no names on the stones but she didn't want to, either.

The cold had now become biting, and Joy found herself shivering. In the distance, the light from the lantern could just make clear a small structure. As Joy drew nearer, she could see that it was a sort of open wooden hut, erected over another headstone. There was a small handful of flowers at the foot of it. Coming closer still, Joy could feel both a great pull and a substantial amount of grief coming from here.

I can't. I can't go any further.
You must. You know you must.

She arrived at the grave. The stone was covered in snow and she could read nothing on it.

Wipe away the snow.
No!!

She needn't have argued with herself. The bobin returned and perched herself grimly on top of the stone. She looked at Joy without an ounce of delight. And Joy knew what the bird was about to do.

'Go on then,' Joy whispered. 'Do what you have to do. I won't blame you.'

As if understanding, Fortune pecked sharply downwards and much of the snow covering the stone fell to the floor at Joy's knees, who now crouched in front of the grave, forcing herself to look at it. The bobin continued her work until enough snow was cleared that a name was clearly visible on the frozen stone.

Cold grief wrapped itself cruelly around her, and Joy could do nothing but let another oncoming memory carry her bleakly away.

~

Lothar was flying. The cool air breezed through his hair as he flew downwards on his sledge, and for just a moment he thought he might crash at the bottom. But he was not afraid. The thought of colliding with something or somebody was thrilling. His heart raced further and he was almost met with disappointment when he landed safely and skidded softly onto the nearby path, lightly spraying a man who was busy with something at the bottom.

'Oi!' the man jeered. 'Watch it, Lothar! You should take your sledge further up that way. You know what we're building here.'

'Sorry Mister Eric,' Lothar said. 'I didn't think you'd be working on it. Not on Christmas Day.' He picked himself up and brushed the snow from his coat.

'We must,' Eric replied, looking at the boy with heavy eyes. 'We can't stop for Christmas. *They* won't stop either, will they?'

Lothar's heart dropped. *They*. He hadn't much of a clue who *they* were. But they were the talk of the village. Had been for almost as long as Lothar could remember. But still, he knew very little of who or what was being referred to.

'Run along now,' Eric said, his attention returning to his task. 'You shouldn't be here. This is no place for a young lad like yourself.'

'I'm ten now, Mister Eric,' Lothar returned, proudly.

'Aye, well ten's still no age to be hanging around in a graveyard. Especially not this one. Now be off with you. And tell your mother I'll pop round with some scones later. Plenty enough for a mother and her three child…'

Eric stopped himself here and screwed his eyes shut painfully.

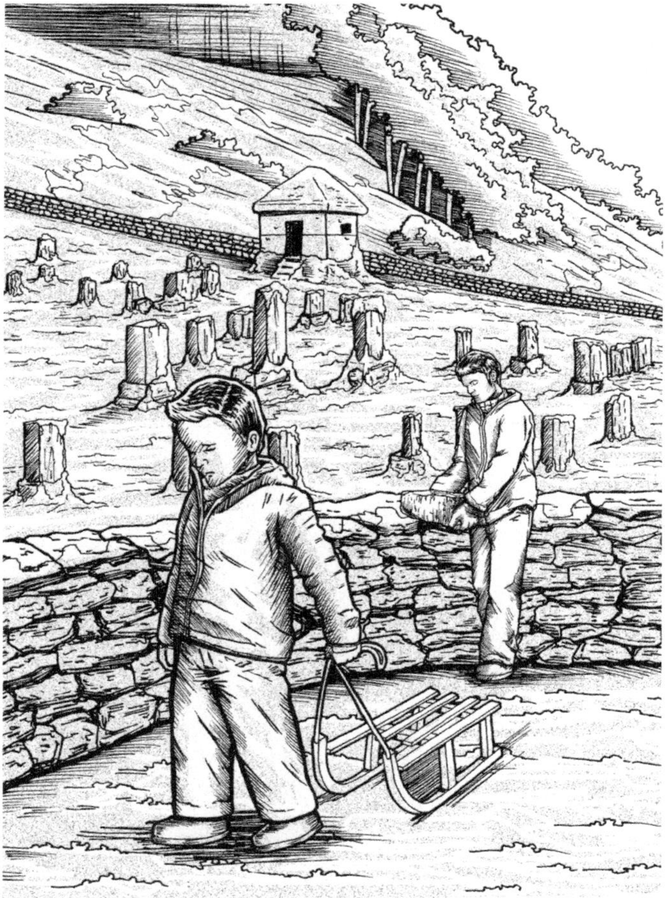

'Ah... What I mean is... Plenty enough for all of you.'

'Okay, Mister Eric,' Lothar said. 'Thank you. And merry Christmas.'

Eric's head fell slightly to one side at this, as though pondering what the boy had meant by *merry Christmas*.

'Aye,' he said eventually. 'Aye, and a merry Christmas to you too, son. And to all of you.'

Lothar drew the rope of his sledge to one shoulder and began dragging it away when Eric called to him once more.

'Lothar!'

The boy turned around and observed a grave and sorrowful look in Eric's eyes.

'I was awful sorry to hear about your father. And your sister. Terrible times we're in.'

Not knowing what to say to this, Lothar broke eye contact with Eric and simply nodded his head before turning away and allowing him to resume building the great wall surrounding the new graveyard.

***

When Lothar returned home, he found Malin chopping vegetables.

'Hello Mother,' he said with a stronger hint of gloom in his voice than he'd intended.

Malin gazed up from the chopping board. A wide smile spread across her tired face.

'Hello, Lothar!' she beamed. 'How was your new sledge?'

'It was good,' Lothar replied. 'Not many other children were there though. I thought there would be loads.'

'There used to be in days gone by,' Malin said, returning her focus to chopping an orange vegetable. 'The numbers have certainly thinned these last few years.'

'I thought Jonas might have joined me,' Lothar said, sadly. He took off his coat and hung it beside the door.

'He might have,' Malin said. 'If he didn't have so much on his mind. Goodness knows we all do. But you know what he's thinking about, Lothar.'

'Yes,' Lothar said. 'I do. Do you want some help?'

Malin smiled all the more widely. 'That would be lovely. Here, you can chop these if you're *very* careful. I doubt any of us want to find your chopped finger in our soup bowl.'

Malin laid out some more of the orange vegetables onto a separate chopping board and handed Lothar a smaller knife than the one she was using. Lothar began chopping the vegetables and then throwing them into the soup pot alongside his mother. For a while, neither of them spoke, but Malin continued to smile.

'Do you think we'll get a message today?' Lothar asked.

The smile faded a little from Malin's face.

'Oh, I don't know dear. I certainly hope so. But it doesn't do to sit and wait for these things. To *expect* them. It's been a hard year, but at least the three of us are together, eh?'

'Where *is* Jonas?' Lothar asked.

'Out in the back. As usual. You haven't really seen him today. Perhaps you should go and wish him a merry Christmas?'

Lothar nodded. His mother's timing was perfect; he had just finished throwing the last of his chopped vegetables into the bubbling pot. Malin thanked him and kissed him softly on the cheek before he left through the front door, ambled past his discarded sledge and made his way to the back of the house.

He found Jonas under the cover of the slanted roof of the house. He was shirtless on the floor practising sit-ups, rocking his body back and forth animatedly, cold breath escaping his lungs and drifting as vapour into the air above. His body had become muscular over the last few months and Lothar wondered why he continued to train. He looked strong enough already. He surely didn't need to be much stronger? Once Jonas finished another six or seven sit-ups, he spotted Lothar approaching.

'Hello, little brother,' he said. 'Merry Christmas.'

'Merry Christmas,' Lothar returned. He stood a few feet from Jonas, watching him continue his exercise. 'It's not *that* merry though. It isn't even snowing.'

Jonas allowed a small smile to form on his mouth. 'Of all the things you could choose to be remorseful over. And you choose to be sad because it isn't snowing for once?'

Lothar couldn't help but smile with his brother, and soon enough the smiles escalated into gentle laughter. Jonas spun himself around and changed his exercise to press-ups.

'Why have you been training so much?' Lothar asked.

Jonas stopped what he was doing. He changed to a sitting position and looked at his little brother with serious and sorrowful eyes.

'I think you know why,' he said.

Lothar walked to the side of Jonas and took a seat on a little wooden bench that their father had built some years ago.

'You're going to fight,' Lothar said, not looking at his brother.

'Yes,' Jonas said softly. 'I have to, Lothar. They'll call me up eventually anyway. I'm an adult now. Of age to fight. Better it's my own decision to go, and not anyone else's. Don't you think?'

Lothar made no reply. He felt a sting in his eyes and a sharp pain in his heart.

'And maybe I'll find Father,' Jonas said, reassuringly. 'Or Annika.'

The mention of his father and sister made Lothar look up at Jonas hopefully. He was desperate. Desperate for any news of the two of them. And for weeks they had heard nothing. All Lothar could do was to either dread their fate or dare to dream that they were somehow together, alive, fighting whatever evil it was that they were enlisted to fight. Maybe even winning.

The brothers sat in silence for a while. The village was quiet, but not entirely silent. Around them, Lothar could hear intermittent chatter, at times even laughter. The number of people who still lived here had dwindled significantly of late, but those who were left seemed at least a little defiant still, determined that the years of war would have little effect on this day, the most special of the year.

Suddenly, Lothar felt a light thud on the top of his head, followed by a cold shiver down the back of his neck. He knew what had happened straight away. Looking up at his brother, he caught him grinning slyly, a small piece of land stripped of snow to his left.

'You good-for-nothing brute!'

He leapt good heartedly from the bench and launching himself into the air, landed with a thud on Jonas' chest who was beside himself with laughter. Jonas tossed him off and he landed with a soft thump into the snowy back garden. Filling his gloved hands with as much snow as he could, Lothar launched it spiritedly towards his brother, who managed to dive away in the nick of time to avoid the collision.

The brothers, chuckling with merriment continued pelting each other with snowballs. Jonas, being much older and fitter than Lothar, had the upper hand, but once or twice Lothar managed to catch him with an excellent shot. At times, his brother was laughing so hard that he could barely summon the energy to throw his snowballs and would instead crouch low to the floor, clutching at his sides as they ached from howling.

This is more like it, Lothar thought. *This is what I thought Christmas was like!*

When they were finally too tired to continue their fight, the boys sat side by side on the wooden bench that Lothar had earlier occupied. Smiling and gasping for breath, Lothar gazed upwards to the sky. The sun would set soon in its brilliant orange-red glow, bringing about the end of another day. He could see that it had already begun its journey downwards and he wondered if perhaps his father or Annika were watching the same sun. How did they celebrate Christmas while at war? Was there even any time to do so? He thought of Mister Eric again, building the wall around the new graveyard. *We can't stop for Christmas. They won't stop either, will they?*

'Look, little brother!'

Jonas' voice interrupted Lothar's thoughts. He was pointing upwards to the sky. At first, Lothar couldn't see what he was pointing to but before long he spotted it; a single white snowflake drifting down to them as slowly and gracefully as a pleasant ballad sung by a lone caroller.

'There you are then,' Jonas smiled. 'You have your snow at Christmas after all.'

Lothar took off the glove from his right hand and reached it out as the single snowflake fell languidly towards it. When it finally reached his hand, Lothar pulled it in towards him and looked at it. It was beautiful. He held it close to him. He could feel the slight chill of it, could almost make out its intricate, starry pattern on his hand.

'The only snowflake of Christmas,' Jonas said, beside him. 'That's a special thing indeed, little brother.'

Yes, it was. A little piece of joy that came floating only to him. A forgotten memory of things past, happy times and happy people. Jolly spirits and wholesome goodwill. Friends, family, food and laughter. All of this, Lothar held in his hand in the form of a snowflake.

But soon, it was gone. Melted away and now simply a part of that memory of bygone times.

'And just like that it disappears,' Lothar said, sadly.

Jonas placed a hand warmly on his little brother's shoulder.

'But at least it was with us, if only for a short while.'

***

The dinner table was merry enough. Malin continued to smile as she ladled large portions of hearty soup into bowls while Jonas cut and buttered the bread. Lothar had been tasked with setting the table and had done well to remember the order in which the knives and forks were placed beside the plates. He arranged the white and red flowers in the vase at the centre of the table so that they beamed out in every direction, spreading their jovial beauty to all sides. At the head of each plate, he placed one of his mother's home-made Christmas crackers.

As they enjoyed their soup, the conversation was focused on happy topics, and steered clear of anything to do with the war. Jonas and Malin both had a talent for jokes and made Lothar laugh heartily and plenty. At one point, Jonas told a joke about grey hair that Lothar didn't quite understand. Malin had playfully thrown her cracker at him after it and Jonas refused Lothar's requests to understand what had been meant by the joke.

After the soup, the family shared generous servings of meat pie, roast potatoes and vegetables of all shapes, colours and descriptions. There were larger portions of everything this year as there were less mouths sharing the food, which was a bleak enough thought for Lothar to keep to himself, yet he wondered how much this was on the minds of his mother and brother.

Malin had taken sole responsibility for the poems in the crackers for her boys, and Jonas had written a humorous but touching one for his mother which had brought a small tear to her eye. It had suddenly felt to Lothar as though all the grief and sorrow which had somehow seemed to have enveloped the village was gone for a moment, and in its place was something which had already been there at the root of it all; family, love, gratitude, and most of all, joy.

The family were visited now and then by many of their fellow villagers bearing gifts. The numbers having significantly diminished over the last few months and years, Malin opted to do the round alone this year so that the boys might find some fun in the house. She hadn't managed to carry everything by herself, however, and resigned to accept that those she couldn't reach would no doubt call at her own home. Presently, Mister Eric had arrived with his promised batch of scones for the family, and by this point Lothar's stomach was so full that he recoiled at the thought of eating any more.

'Here you are, Eric,' Malin said to him, kissing him lightly on the cheek and handing him a thin woollen scarf. 'It's not much I'm afraid, times being as they are.'

'Not at all, Malin,' Eric answered. 'It's the giving of the gifts and not the gifts themselves that bring the purest of joy.'

As he said this, Lothar thought that Eric's face contained not even the faintest spark of what he would name *joy*. Nonetheless, Eric called over to the boys, wishing them a merry Christmas before wrapping his new scarf around him and heading back out into the cold evening.

Something odd happened then. As soon as the door had closed and Malin had returned to the table, a pronounced silence fell upon them. As Malin had been speaking at the door, Jonas had been building a fire, and the usually quiet and calming cracks of the wood were somehow louder and more ominous. They all surely felt it, Lothar thought. Those loud snaps from the fireplace had seemed to take a life of their own, and with every one of them came some sort of distant warning.

Malin's smile had now disappeared. Joining them at the table, Jonas kept his head turned down to the wood beneath it. Lothar simply looked into the fire, stared deeply inside it as though daring it to communicate with them, tell them all what secrets it knew.

The silence perhaps becoming too insufferable, Malin drew in a breath to speak but was stopped by a knocking at the door.

Lothar knew at once. He knew that the caller outside was different to the others who had been coming through the evening. Something about the way the person had knocked had exuded a heaviness, a mournful reluctance, as though the knocker had not wished to knock at all. Even the way that Malin stood up slowly and drew her chair back hesitantly told Lothar that she too somehow knew that she *must* answer the door, but that in doing so she would be bringing a darkness into this, the most cheerful and cherished day of the year.

After swinging the door open, and before either Lothar or Jonas could see who was at the other end of it, Malin placed both hands to her mouth and gasped, eyes widely staring outside.

'Hello, Malin,' came a man's voice. Lothar didn't recognise it. 'May I come in?'

Malin stood for a moment, unmoving and silent before finally crying, 'Lars! For all that is good in this world, I did not expect to see you on this day! Yes, come in, come in. Sit yourself by the fire, you look frozen half to death!'

At the mention of Lars' name, Jonas had swiftly stood up and was now looking at the door frame as a large man carrying a great brown sack limped inside and looked over to him.

'Jonas, my lad,' Lars remarked. 'You've gotten so tall. And this surely cannot be little Lothar!'

'Lars!' Jonas breathed. 'But why are you here?'

'In good time, Jonas, my love,' Malin said, closing the door behind her and rushing over to the table to make a space for Lars. 'Let the man settle himself in and we'll no doubt hear his story when it is ready to be told. Have you eaten, Lars? There's plenty of food, still. I'll warm up the soup. Jonas, fetch the beer from the kitchen. Lothar, take Lars' coat and hang it over there. Are you hurt, Lars? We have bandages and a little medicine.'

While his mother fussed over this tall man, Lothar did as instructed and took Lars' heavy, soggy coat to hang it up. He remembered the man only very vaguely. He was a jolly sort of fellow and used to live just two doors down from them. He was a good friend of their father's...

By the time Lothar had returned to the table, Malin had set him a seat right by the fire. Jonas poured three beers and set them on the table in front of himself, his mother and Lars.

'And what about the boy?' Lars asked. 'I've lost a little sense of time lately but I believe today is Christmas. Surely the boy can have a drop of beer?'

Lothar grinned pertly at this and Malin reluctantly agreed, pouring a small amount of beer into the mug which had previously contained some milk that Lothar had finished. Sipping it carefully, Lothar found that it wasn't to his taste, but swiftly kept his grimace from Jonas, who was watching him with some interest.

Malin had a bowl of soup in front of Lars quicker than Lothar would have expected, alongside the last of the bread. Lars thanked her gratefully before tucking in and finishing the soup almost as quickly as it had been served.

'I brought gifts for you all,' Lars said, indicating towards the sack he had placed by the table. 'Perhaps you can distribute them, Jonas?'

Jonas leaned over and brought the sack to him. Reaching a hand in, he pulled out a most peculiar object. It was a silver toy made from metal and in the shape of a dragon, but around it were several cogs. On the dragon's left side was a large but thin piece of metal.

'That one is for Lothar. Put it on the table, Jonas,' Lars said. Jonas did as he was asked, and Lars leaned his large frame over the table before reaching out to the toy, groaning and wincing as he did so. Keeping one hand on the dragon, he used the other to wind the extended piece of metal. It made a clunking kind of sound as he did so.

A key of some sort, Lothar thought.

Lars released the toy now and Lothar saw Jonas join him in marvelling at what happened next. The dragon began moving by itself, using its metal legs to propel itself forwards and swaying its head to and fro, as though searching for enemies. Once its head had swung once each to the left and right the dragon stopped walking and moved its head upwards, staring at the ceiling. Lothar could imagine a deep, loud roar shaking the house.

'What spectacle!' Malin cried. 'How in the name of all things good does it work!'

'Well don't stop there, Jonas!' Lars said after taking a swig of beer. 'Reach in again and see what else there is.'

Jonas reached in and this time pulled out a square, metal box.

'Ah, that one's for you, Malin,' Lars said.

Jonas passed it to his mother who began inspecting it. She found that the top half of the box slid open, and inside was a small compartment with two paddles attached to a wheel of some sort. Malin found a lever which turned these paddles as she moved it.

'It's for making dough,' Lars said. 'I've seen them used once or twice. You just put all your ingredients inside and let the machine knead for you. No need to get your hands dirty.'

Malin smiled at Lars. 'How wonderful! Thank you, Lars.'

Lars looked to Jonas, somewhat more forbiddingly than before. 'Just the final one now. Go ahead, Jonas. The last one's for you.'

Jonas paused for a brief moment before reaching in. He did this slowly, and when his hand reached the final item in the sack, instead of pulling it out he unravelled the sack around the item, and the mood in the room lost any spark of joviality it had previously clung on to.

Lars took another large swig of beer while Malin sat, open-mouthed at the item in her eldest son's hands. Lothar knew what it was too, and quickly looked away, as though he may get in trouble just for glancing at it.

'Believe me boy,' Lars said. 'You'll need it.'

Without saying a word, Jonas placed the rifle carefully onto the table next to Lothar's dragon.

'Don't worry, it's not loaded,' Lars assured.

Malin stared at the gun, apparently lost for words. Lars cleared his throat.

'It's important that I tell you all I have no news of Sander. None at all,' he said. Lothar and Jonas' heads sprung up at the sound of their father's name, and their eyes fixed on Lars. 'But I fear you may be receiving news very shortly. I came here straight from the war.'

'How does it fare?' Jonas asked, promptly. Malin looked at Lars. The tension in the room was thickened.

Lars looked sadly at Jonas. 'It's difficult to say. Some days we were told we were gaining ground.

Others, our commanders seemed to have completely vanished. But all the while there was always this feeling of... *dread* around that battlefield. A constant sadness surrounding the place, making it difficult to think clearly. And the ones we're fighting, they... They seem to lack all emotion. They know no fear or sadness, no happiness nor hope. One of them shot me, and I was sent home to recover. I'm sure I'll be called back soon enough.'

Another silence fell upon the room until finally Malin spoke again.

'You said you feared we may receive news soon. What makes you think this?'

This time, Lars emptied his mug before speaking.

'Shortly after I arrived at the village, I saw a caravan. I know the type and I'm sure you do too. It was carrying...'

Here, Lars paused and glanced at Lothar for a moment before drawing his eyes away and staring instead into the fire.

'Well, it was carrying unfortunate souls. Ones destined for that new place they're still building the wall for. But also in that caravan was a messenger.'

Lothar sharply drew in a breath. Before he could help himself, he blurted out a question for Lars. 'Has the messenger been going around the houses?'

It seemed as though Lars had to force himself to bring his eyes painfully away from the fire and rest them uneasily on Lothar.

'Yes. Yes, he has.'

Lothar sprang from the table, ignoring Malin's plea for him to stay where he was. He ran to the window and gazed out of it, searching for this messenger. Only around half of the lanterns were lit again tonight, and he could barely make anything out through the black darkness.

Drat it! Where is he?

'Lothar, my love…' Malin started, but she was unable to finish. Four sharp and ominous knocks came at the door.

'Lothar, go back to the table,' Malin commanded in a much firmer tone. She had risen from the table and was now walking quickly towards the front door. '*Now,* please.'

Lothar returned to the table, shaking. Jonas and Lars equally had their heads turned to the front door which was now open. They could not see the person but they could hear his low, muffled voice as he spoke to Malin. Lothar could make out no words, but he thought, hopefully, that the tone of his voice sounded reassuring.

When Malin closed the front door, she held in her hands an envelope. Standing where she was, she tore it open, pulled out a single piece of paper and read.

After what seemed to Lothar an eternity, he witnessed his mother screw her face up, fight back tears, stroll forcefully towards the table and wordlessly hand the paper to Jonas. Lothar stood and read it over his brother's shoulder.

Dear Malin,

It is with the deepest of regret that I write to inform you that your husband Sander was yesterday killed fighting the enemy. He fought very bravely and will be remembered here as a valued soldier, and an honourable man.

I am sorry to have to bring you this news during Christmas, and I will be thinking of your family at this difficult time. My only reassurance to you is that I believe his death not to be in vain. Your husband dedicated his last remaining days to fighting back against an enemy that we will defeat.

With deepest condolences and best wishes,

Captain EJ Aland

Jonas dropped the letter to the table and went instantly to his mother. Malin had been fine until her eldest son wrapped his arms tightly around her, at which point, grief took her sharply by the throat and she wept cold tears into Jonas' chest. Lars simply sat at the table, staring into the fire, knowing full well what the news was without having to read the letter.

Lothar felt nothing at first. A strange sort of emptiness took over and he stood plainly, watching his mother and Jonas openly sob.

I'm a monster, he thought. *I should be sad like Jonas and Mother. Why don't I feel sad? Why don't I feel anything at all?*

Why?

***

Malin regained enough composure to see Lothar to bed later on in the night. She lovingly tucked him in warmly and kissed him on the forehead before blowing out the candle in his room and leaving with a sad smile.

It was the first Christmas night of Lothar's life that his mother hadn't sang him a carol.

3
2000 Light Years

This time, Joy was flying. Soaring through the air and dodging in and out of the falling snowflakes as swiftly as a bolt of lightning. She felt the crisp air brush past her body and cool her gently as she went.

She perched on her favourite branch and gazed curiously at the scene below. Three people. Two men and a woman. They exited one of the houses and now slowly dawdled through the thick snow and into the darkness beyond.

Is that the last of them?

It would be quiet now. The place would never be the same again. Ah well. Everything must come to an end sooner or later. At least there would still be berries.

Her tiny stomach rumbled at the thought. She fluttered from the branch and soared in the direction of the forest to look for berries.

And then Joy realised. It wasn't real. Or, at least it *was* real some time ago but now it was a distant echo of a memory searching its way through time, hoping not to be lost like so many others.

A fleeting dream.

***

SANDER

The name on the headstone was now slightly covered in snow, but still readable. It was the first thing Joy saw when she came to and it hit her in the stomach like a hard punch.

She sat in Sander's enclosure hugging her knees to her chest and staring at the stone. Her heart had sunk so low into an ocean of anguish that she was sure it would now be irretrievably lost among the black waters of loneliness. It would take the bravest and heartiest of fishermen to find it, but even then, why would they? Why would anyone agree to salvage the heart of a woman who had left behind her little sister? The woman who had stolen and then broken a spacecraft only to wander around a frozen and deserted planet for a little while and then die in a corner next to the grave of a man who would surely have shaken his head at her, turn to his youngest and say to him: *son, if ever you had turned out like that, I would be ashamed.*

Because yes, she was to die here. It seemed everyone else here had anyway, so she might as well join them. What use was she? What use to anyone in this world or the one she came from? Nineteen years of age and her greatest achievement was working in the observation department as a glorified personal assistant. Helping those with greater talents to map out the universe and watch as more primitive peoples discovered fire or electricity. But really, she didn't even watch this; she watched her superiors watch them, and noted that every day their interest dwindled that little bit more until the day came when they had discovered this frozen place and it hadn't even been so much as named. Everyone was too sad by then to notice anything. Nobody was interested when Joy had told them that she'd felt a pull coming from the planet, and that she was absolutely sure that it had everything to do with this great cloud of grief overcoming everyone. Her suggestion of sending a qualified pilot there had been met with a simple shrug of the shoulders and a *let's just see about mapping out that area of Mhyrran with the two new islands.*

Flying that spacecraft and beginning her futile search had been the last stretch of ambition that Joy had had in her. Time to sleep now, and dream of nothing but emptiness and desolation.

***

As her eyes closed, the radio suddenly sparked into life once more.

HOPE CALLING

Joy's heart instantly leapt and she pressed the button on the radio to accept the call.

'Hope? Hope! Can you hear me?'

No sound on the other end.

'Hope?'

She looked at the screen. The signal was lost. Hope must have caught it at a flash of a moment where enough signal had been available for a call.

She felt like throwing the radio to the ground. She felt like tearing her hair out of her head. She felt like standing and screaming in a rage so powerful that it would shatter the branches of the trees surrounding the village.

And then she was calm again. She was herself again. The same Joy who had set off from her home planet to find the cure for sadness for the good of everyone in the universe.

Because she realised that if she was still capable of feeling all of that, some hope remained somewhere inside of her, after all.

***

She turned to Sander's grave once more, kissed the fingers of her gloved hand and then touched it lightly to the stone.

'Goodbye, my friend,' she said. 'I never got to meet you, even though I feel I did know you. Rest forever at peace.'

She turned to leave, but stopped. Facing the grave once more, she spoke again.

'Lothar loved you dearly.'

Because oh, how he did. Joy had felt the boy's emotion deep within her as though it was her own. He was confused, yes. Just like Joy had been when her own parents had left. Confusion and a lack of all other feelings was how it started. Anger followed. How *dare* they leave? How dare they walk out on two young girls who needed them? She began to feel glad they had done so. Good riddance. She felt Lothar probably felt much of the same later in his life.

How dare you go to war, Father. Especially when you had so many who loved you and needed you. You knew there was a risk you wouldn't return but you went anyway. Who cares that you were called? You could have said no. You could have refused.

The very definition of selfishness!

And for Joy, the anger was finally replaced by grief. Grief that she'd kept hidden from Hope. Grief that no doubt Lothar would have kept staunchly secret from Jonas and Malin.

If they had stuck around...

'Stop it!' Joy cried aloud, as though it was anyone else's but her own fault that she was painting an image of Lothar as a resentful and bitter boy, and that he and Joy were very much the same person.

She closed her eyes and took a deep breath. Finally turning from the headstone, she walked once more into the dim graveyard.

It was still snowing heavily. Going in no particular direction, feeling no significant pull, she shuffled forwards into the cold, keeping her head down and her eyes away from the headstones for fear of coming across more names. Names such as *Malin* or *Jonas, or Annika.*

Or Lothar.

She didn't even truly know why seeing Sander's name on the stone had filled her with such sorrow. She was still completely unaware of how long ago these memories of Lothar's were. For all Joy knew, the war might have begun and ended hundreds of years ago. Lothar's family may be dead, but so was anyone who had lived such a long time ago.

But it was still sad. Sad to see the ghosts of the past live so merrily and then be overcome with this dreadfulness. We all must die, yes. But if the journey there is filled with happiness and love between our fellow passengers then we have all lived lives worth living.

A small thud on Joy's right shoulder was enough to cheer her spirits, if only a little.

'Hello, Fortune!' she smiled. 'Where have you been?'

The bird was chirping loudly and pointing her yellow beak back through the gate and towards the village, where Joy saw a remarkable thing.

'Is that... is that a *light* coming from the window of that house?'

She wasn't alone, after all.

***

If she had been asked, Joy would have found it difficult to describe how she felt while walking to the house with the light. Intimidated, perhaps, because she hadn't come across any other people on this planet thus far, and had little way of knowing what they were like. Times, it was clear, had moved hauntingly on from the memories of Lothar long ago. Those cheerful, good-natured villagers from then may have become much different people now. Perhaps it wasn't even *those* people at all; who was to say that the village hadn't been conquered by those others from the war?

So yes, *intimidated* may have been an accurate way of describing how Joy felt. But that wasn't all. She felt intrigued, surprised and even happy. She'd dreaded she might have been the only living person on this entire planet, and then out of the darkness a signal fire was lit, crying out to Joy *this way! Don't lose hope just yet!*

That was it. Hopeful. She felt hopeful. And that was powerful indeed.

The house sat at the top of a small hill. Joy climbed it now, puffing heavily as she marched through the snow. Two posts stood to each side with ropes tied from them to the house. Joy thought that perhaps some of those colourful lanterns were supposed to hang here, but the ropes hung frozen and bare, with no light to cheer them up.

The trek was enough to warm her as she went, and she realised with a little horror that she had allowed her body to become cold and rigid as she'd sat by Sander's grave. Just moments ago, she'd been prepared to die there. Now she'd found another reason to go on.

She reached the house and paused. Should she knock? Or just enter? Suddenly the nerves and intimidation had set in again. Walking to the side of the door and stopping at the window that the light protruded from, she peered inside. She saw a stark room and a lit fireplace. And at the other side of the room, a bed.

Lying on the bed was a man.

Joy stood, frozen, staring at this person on the bed. He was lying with his head pointed to the window. It was difficult to see his face from here.

Is he alive?

He was as still and rigid as the mountain on the other side of the village. Even Fortune, to Joy's side stood with her little eyes fixed on the man, enquiringly. Joy could find no evidence of breathing. But he surely must have lit the fireplace? It looked fresh. The fire was burning in large, orange and red flames.

She decided it would be best to go inside. Perhaps see if this man was still alive, check whether he needed some help. She walked back to the front door, tried the handle, and found that the door swung open easily. She stepped inside. Taking no time to notice anything particular about her surroundings, she turned left and entered the door to the room with the stranger.

It was warm in here. The fire had certainly done its job. For the first time since arriving here, Joy felt like taking her coat off. She looked at the man on the bed. Still, lifeless. Like most other places Joy had been to in her life, she found that this room was encased with grief.

Fortune flew to the fire's mantelpiece. It would no doubt be cosy there. Joy took her coat off and let it flop softly to the floor. She walked quietly to the man's bed, heart fluttering wildly.

'Hello? Sir?'

No response.

She knelt by the bed and looked at the man's face. He was old. Grey hair and many lines on his face which, Joy thought, were likely not just from the passage of time. Each line told a story of unhappiness or war. She hoped that perhaps others told of happier times.

And then she felt it. A tiny piece of her Sense was trying to tell her something. Not a memory, just a reminder of sorts. She saw Lothar again, in a place she'd seen him before. Ten years old and dragging his sledge sadly away from a man building a wall.

'Eric!' Joy gasped.

His eyes quivered open.

For a moment, their eyes locked and no words were spoken. Eric's face had little expression on it. Joy was sure her own was full of shock.

'You know me, young girl?' Eric said, finally.

Joy nodded. 'Yes.'

Eric looked at her, thoughtfully. 'But I don't recall your face. What's your name?'

'Joy. My name is Joy.'

Eric snorted. 'That can't be true. There's no such thing as *joy*. Not anymore.'

'Are you okay?' Joy asked. 'Are you hurt? Can I help you?'

Eric raised his eyebrows. 'Help me, dear girl? Nobody wants to help anyone else these days. You must have come a very long way.'

'Further than you would imagine,' Joy said.

'Aye,' Eric agreed. 'I can tell as much by your strange garments.'

As he spoke, there was very little feeling in Eric's words. He spoke absently, as though he was asleep and talking to nobody in particular. His eyes drifted off to the ceiling now, where they sadly settled.

'What happened here?' Joy asked. 'Where is everyone?'

'Don't you know?' Eric asked. 'They're all gone.'

'Where?' Joy asked. She tried to keep her voice soft as she spoke. 'Where did everyone go?'

Eric simply sighed, and said nothing.

'Do you know a man named Lothar?' Joy asked. This seemed to draw Eric's attention back to her.

'Lothar?' he repeated. 'Aye, I do. I do. Gone up to the mountain, he did.'

'The mountain?' Joy said, hopefully. 'Why?'

'Trying to find something.'

'Trying to find what?'

'Joy.'

Another pause. The only sound in the room was the warm crackling from the fireplace.

Finally, Eric broke the silence.

'I'm dying, you know.'

Joy had no words to say to this. How does a person respond when they've just been told something like this? Perhaps she might have given the man some comforting words, but he didn't seem particularly perturbed at the fact that he was departing. He'd given Joy the news with little emotion in his voice, as though he was simply commenting on the weather. Thinking of nothing else to say, Joy asked Eric a question.

'How?'

Eric looked at her. 'Oh, the same way everyone's going these days. The grief got to me.'

'You can die from... sadness?' Joy asked.

'If you're sad *enough*,' Eric responded. 'Hasn't this been happening where you come from?'

It had, in a way. The population in Gylfandell had been thinning for years, and Joy knew well enough that many had succumbed to their depression and chosen grim fates too terrible to speak of. It was shocking at first, but the people had gotten used to it, and every new death reported had been talked of with less surprise and more indifference. But Joy had never heard of a person lying in bed and literally dying from their own grief.

'Can't I do something for you?' Joy asked, holding back a doleful tear or two. 'Can't I help you?'

'Can't I rest?' Eric replied. 'Can't I have peace?'

Joy took Eric's hand in her own. The tears fell silently down her cheeks now. Gracefully, Fortune flew from the mantelpiece and landed soundlessly on Eric's chest.

'If peace is what you choose then you shall have it,' Joy whispered. 'Rest, Eric. Would you like me to stay with you?'

She could only see Eric's face through shadows warmly lit by the fire, but she thought and chose to believe that she could see a gentle smile form on the man's face.

'Yes,' Eric said. 'Yes, stay. And tell me of where you come from.'

Joy told him all she could of her city. She told him of the great size of the place, the tall buildings, the bustling streets, the noises and the smells and the sights. Eric listened silently, asking no questions and giving no sign that he was hearing anything of what Joy was saying. And as she spoke, Fortune stayed on Eric's chest. At first, the bobin had been peering into Eric's face quizzically, popping her head back and forth. Now she sat, puffed up and comfortable, eyes half-closed but never moving away from the man.

Finally, Joy stopped talking, and saw that Eric had stopped breathing. She bent over him and softly kissed his hand before gently placing it to his side. Wiping at her eyes, she stood and spoke quietly.

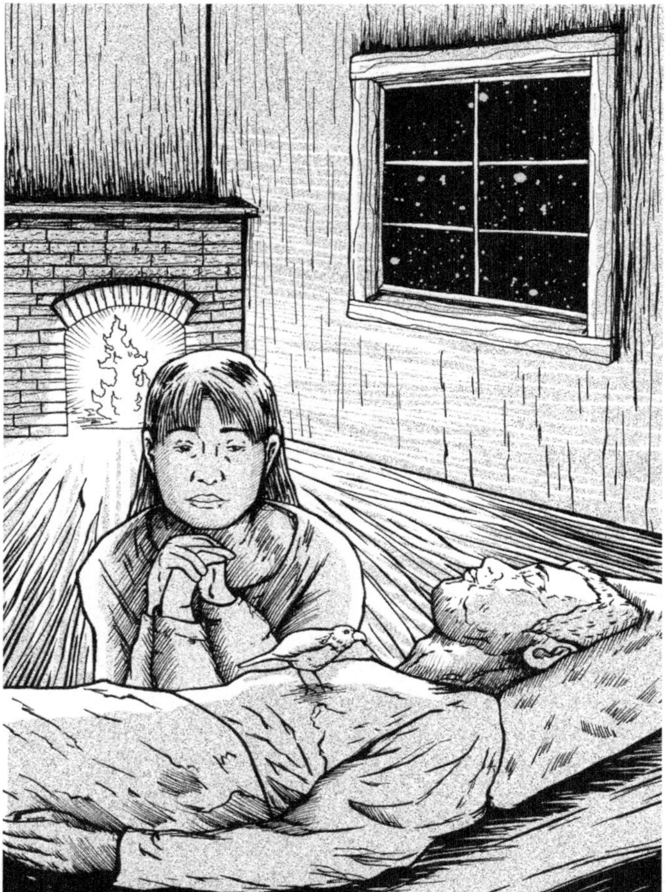

'This is not death. This is peace.'

And even Fortune seemed to unloose a silver tear of her own.

***

The mountain.

She now had a definite target, and an idea of just how old Lothar's memories were. He was alive. Or, at least had been the last time Eric had seen him. And he'd climbed the mountain in search for joy. Did he know something? Had he discovered what Joy's own Sense had been pointing towards?

But she didn't know *when* Lothar had gone to the mountain. Had no idea how far up he had made it. Did he even have any idea of what to do when he got there?

The only thing she could do now was to put her coat and gloves back on and make for the mountain.

Lothar may have been searching for joy, but Joy was also searching for him.

***

The night had gotten colder. The snow still fell, but a little lighter now, fluttering down towards the village as though the snowflakes were children sneaking up on their giggling friends and trying to frighten them. Fortune flew ahead of Joy, pointing the way towards the mountain.

'Don't worry, Fortune,' Joy said. 'I see it.'

They passed the stone wall of the graveyard, the lonely Christmas tree with its ancient, frozen decorations and many houses that had been left to be buried by the snow. As she walked through the village,

Joy began to see forgone and forlorn ghosts; silent memories of people long gone from here in the days before the sadness came. They lit up the area like desolate lanterns, poignant smiles stretched across their faces as they wandered the streets and spoke voicelessly to their neighbours. And Joy knew. She could almost hear their voices confirming it.

Hallo, my fine fellow! It's Christmas Day! Clash, clang, hammer, ding, dong, bell. Oh, glorious, glorious!

The baker and the lumberjack exchanged gifts underneath the great tree. The cook and the tailor shared wine with the musicians before they began their mute songs. The village was once again enshrined in happiness.

But just like Lothar's snowflake, it faded and disappeared into the night, leaving Joy with a clear view of Fortune as she sailed through the air towards the awaiting mountain.

***

The village was behind her now. Joy slogged on through the thick snow and kept her eyes fixed on the mountain in front of her. Fortune had come back to her now and settled in her usual place on Joy's shoulder. It comforted her.

'Whatever we face tonight, we face together.'

There had to be a way to bring joy back. There had to. The universe would die without it. Just like poor Eric. Joy knew the memory of seeing him die of nothing else than sadness would haunt her for the rest of her life. What if she was to die in this way?

What if Hope was to die in this way?

Troublesome, unhelpful thought. Hope would not die like that. Not on Joy's watch. Even if she could never see her sister again, she would at least restore her happiness. She would help her smile again.

Presently, Joy felt a sudden sensation of approaching darkness. A feeling of dread quietly announced itself, and she was sure Fortune could feel it too, because the bird began softly chirping with a nervous tone.

She knew instantly what it was.

She stopped and whispered to the bobin. 'Fortune. Stay with me. Don't fly away from it. I won't let anything happen to you.'

And as usual, Fortune seemed to perfectly understand her. She went rigid; afraid but unmoving, sitting as calmly as she could manage on Joy's shoulder and awaiting whatever terror it was that had been pursuing them. But then, perhaps Fortune had already been aware of this thing. Maybe that was why she was so afraid of it. Could it be that the bird was scared because she knew she had good reason to be?

Joy heard it now. Footsteps. Not rushing like before, at Lothar's old house. This time the dark thing moved more slowly, more measuredly. It didn't sound as though it was sneaking up on Joy and Fortune; its footsteps rang out loudly from behind them, announcing their arrival proudly. Joy took a deep breath and turned around.

She saw a huge black frame. A creature with narrow eyes that glinted in the night as they stared forwards. A set of razor-sharp white teeth within an open mouth that looked ready to snap. It walked on all fours, head pointed down towards the snow.

A black wolf. But this one was impossibly enormous compared with any that Joy had seen back home. Perhaps these were called something entirely different here. Or maybe this was the common size of what Joy understood to be a wolf. Either way, it was truly terrifying.

'Stay back,' Joy commanded with a trembling voice. She'd been so used to speaking to Fortune, she had no hesitation to speak now to this animal.

The wolf grinned.

'You... you're smiling,' Joy gasped. 'You understand me, Wolf?'

'My name is not *Wolf*,' it returned. 'I like to be known as *Hunter*.'

Joy nearly fell to her knees at the sound of the wolf's voice. It was deep and menacing yet slow and calm.

'You can *talk?*' Joy said.

The wolf said nothing in response to this, but its grin widened. On Joy's shoulder, Fortune was shaking. The wolf now began walking slowly around them, circling them. It sniffed the air.

'I've lost the scent. Someone nearby was fading. It wasn't you, was it?'

'I...' Joy began. 'I don't know what you mean.'

The wolf snorted. 'You're not from around here, are you?'

Joy said nothing. She stood stiffly, keeping her eyes focused on the wolf, turning as it went to go behind her.

It laughed.

'What's so funny?' Joy demanded in as firm a voice as she could manage.

'You,' the wolf said, continuing to smile. 'You're very on edge. What are you so afraid of?'

'That you might attack us,' Joy said, deciding to be honest with the creature. 'That you might eat us.'

'Eat *you?*' the wolf said. 'Don't be foolish. I can't eat you. Not yet.'

Not yet. What did this thing mean by *not yet?* As though sensing Joy's thoughts, the wolf answered this question.

'I feed from those who have lost all hope of ever being joyful again. It's how I thrive.'

Then Joy understood. The wolf had caught the scent of Eric, and then lost it when he had passed.

'Then you have nothing to find here, Wolf,' Joy said.

The wolf's grin vanished. 'I told you my name is Hunter.'

'Is that a name you chose for yourself?' Joy asked, feeling a little braver. 'Because if I were you, I might have chosen another. One that suits you better. Misery, perhaps.'

'You think me an evil thing?' the wolf asked.

'You feed on those who have lost their happiness. The ones who have no hope of it returning to them. Yes, I think you evil.'

'Aahhhh…' the wolf sighed. Its smile returned moderately to its face. 'You think I'm responsible for the loss of joy?'

She had. Something about this monster felt entirely wrong. That feeling of oncoming dread when it was around had suggested to Joy that she'd found the cause of the universe's suffering. Had she really been mistaken?

'What are you?' Joy demanded.

'I am Hunter,' the wolf returned. 'A happy beneficiary from the current situation. Exactly what I am you will not understand. Until it's time for me to feed from you. And that time *will* come. Oh, yes it will come! And you are so *young*. How I love to feed from the youth. Especially children. But it has been some time since I have had the pleasure of finding one.'

Joy felt sick. 'You are evil indeed. Go back to whatever hole you climbed out of.'

'In time, I will,' the wolf said. 'And I will take you with me.'

Suddenly, its grin disappeared once more. It sniffed the air eagerly, seeming to catch another scent. It threw its head back and howled awfully into the night. The sound rang out and stung Joy's ears. She covered them with her hands. When the wolf finished, it darted off, sending tufts of snow from the ground into the air as it went.

Oh no, Joy thought. *It's caught the scent of someone else.*

Hunter sped towards the mountain.

***

She moved forwards with more urgency now. The wolf had left deep tracks in the snow that were easy to see, even in the darkness. By now, the clouds had cleared a little and Joy could see two moons. They were close to this planet and shone enough light for her to see her surroundings in enough detail. The mountain wasn't far now. She couldn't outrun the wolf, but she could perhaps stay very close behind. And it would have to rely on its sense of smell to find its prey. Joy had her own Sense, one that the wolf was completely unaware of. And she had a feeling that this may have been more powerful than the wolf's nose.

Fortune had taken to stretching her wings again, flying a little in front of Joy and stopping on the branch of a nearby tree or a snow-covered rock, waiting for her to catch up. When she did, the bobin would flutter off again and find another place to land and watch Joy as she tirelessly urged herself forwards, forwards, never slowing, perpetually pushing on, raising her head occasionally only to see how close the foot of the mountain was.

It was here.

Without noticing, Joy had been clambering up the lowest part of it and was now very much climbing upwards. Looking behind her she could see the village. It was lit up in lights of green and red. She could hear laughter coming from deep within.

Ghosts. More ghosts. The ghosts of Christmases long past.

And as she watched the lights fade and become the lost village that she had come to know, Joy asked herself if she perhaps now knew the settlement as well as any man, woman, child or even bobin who had set foot or wing there.

Know it! I could walk it blindfold...

As the lights faded and became darkness once more, Joy could hear the singing of long ago. A choir, singing a carol of some sort. She had never heard the song before but she knew in her heart that it was supposed to sound jolly. It didn't. It sounded as though the fact that it was now a long distant memory of a thing called *happiness* had nothing at all to do with it being sung by ghosts. That's what they always were. Spirits lamenting an absent idea of a legend named joy.

Gaudete, gaudete Christus est natus
Ex maria virgine, gaudete

And just like the lights, the voices slowly faded and allowed the wind to carry them off to some forgotten shore where they slept for aye.

Memory... Joy thought, lethargically. *There's a memory coming...*

But I can't stop now! The wolf. Lothar.
It's another strong one.

Got to keep going.

Impossible. The memory is coming whether you want it to or not. Find shelter, if you can.

Collapsing to a part of the ground where the snow was thinner and resting her back against a large tree which provided limited cover from the gentle snowdrops was all Joy could manage before being once again swept off to the past.

~

Lothar woke early. The sun had barely poked its head past the great mountain before the baby began crying. The child's mother assured her husband that she would attend to the matter. She stretched and walked to the baby's room.

'Oh dear, what's the matter, my child?' The mother's voice was soothing to the baby's ears. The baby calmed a little but continued to gently sob.

Hungry! Need milk!

The mother picked the child up and walked to a wooden chair by the cot where she saw to the matter of feeding.

It was no use. Lothar was awake now. Better he spend these precious first few moments of the day with his beloved wife and daughter. He walked through to the baby's room.

Wordlessly, he smiled coolly and pulled up a chair to sit at his wife's side. She sleepily placed a hand on his leg and leaned her head on his shoulder. He placed a hand of his own on top of hers and the pair simply sat quietly with the baby as she sucked at her mother's breast and the sun began to light up the room in a mellow orange.

'Merry Christmas, Yunie,' Lothar said to his daughter. To his side, a tear fell from his wife's cheek and onto his bare neck, sending a calm note of melancholy into his spirit.

***

'The paths aren't clear again,' Freyja said, looking out of the window. The sky was overcast but it wasn't snowing yet. It had blizzarded the previous night and some of the houses had been completely covered. In years past there had been no shortage of men and women keen to take to the streets to clear the snow from them and make the paths easily seen and walked upon. These days were very different.

Lothar joined Freyja at the window. 'Aye.'

'Are you going to clear ours today?' Freyja asked, absently.

The shovel was leaning against the cold fireplace. He'd looked it out yesterday with the intent of going out to make the path from their house to the Christmas tree safe. Some hope that others would follow suit and clear more paths still lingered somewhere inside him.

'I will,' Lothar said. 'I'll do it after breakfast.'

Breakfast was meagre. Dry bread that had gone a little stale with flavourless jam that Lothar had made from the few wild berries that were to be found on the bush in the garden. It seemed that even plants had given up hope of late. Freyja made tea to go with this, but had almost run out of the nettles she'd been using to make it, and so the drink was nothing much more than hot water. Neither of them finished their mugs.

Yunie sat with them, staring at her parents in wonder. Her wide blue eyes shone as happily as the old lanterns outside. She looked as though she questioned the sudden silence in the room after breakfast had finished. Why weren't her parents talking?

Lothar looked to his daughter. 'She's spending her first Christmas in the same house that I did.'

Freyja's face remained still. She didn't look towards her husband. 'Yes. And all other Christmases after that.'

The words sunk into Lothar slowly but painfully sharply. He had pleasant memories of Christmases past in this house, the one that had once belonged to his parents. But those that had come after the death of his father had been bitter. Jonas had barely rung in the new year before heading out for the first available train that would speed him to war. The Christmas after that had been quiet; only Lothar and his mother. And by the year after that one, when Lothar had been but twelve years old, Malin had been called to the fighting and Lothar hadn't seen her since. He hadn't seen *any* of them, but he would receive the occasional letter which would bring some relief and satisfaction at the finding out that his family were still alive, but also a shrill and profound loneliness.

Taking pity on him, other families had offered Lothar a place at their dinner tables for Christmas Day, and he had found some cheer on these occasions, even if it was tainted by the loss of every person he had ever loved. But as joyous as any of these instances were, he'd always skulk back to his old home and lie in a cold and empty house which had once been so filled with love, but now sat empty and forlorn in an absent sea of pensive echoes.

And then there was the year he had met Freyja. He was a young man by then, hardened by the years of isolation but still as keen somewhere deep inside of him to live and laugh as fully and as heartily as he had in his youth. Freyja had moved into the village after the loss of most of her family, who were now all buried in the graveyard that Lothar had used to gleefully slide down. Her mother had died when their hometown had been attacked. She was trying to shield Freyja's little brother from a shower of flame and ash before it had consumed them both. Devastated by the loss of his wife, Freyja's father had joined the war alongside both of her remaining grandparents. All three of them had been killed.

Freyja's uncle had been instructed to find somewhere safe for her, and here they had stayed ever since. But even after all of this tragedy, Freyja had found the time and patience to smile. And Lothar knew that it wasn't just for herself that she did this; her smile was a courageous act of love for her fellow folk that was intentionally let loose in a thick forest of anguish, a buoyant beacon to signal that although it may be small, hope was not yet gone. Lothar admired her deeply for it.

But as with all things, the years had not been kind to Freyja. Day by day, her smile had lost just a tiny amount of its glow until there was no smile at all. Even after the birth of Yunie who, Lothar knew, Freyja loved as deeply as any mother loved her child, the joy was gone and replaced by a heavy and immovable chain that fixed to her and would not allow her to move from this profound place of despondency.

Presently, Lothar stood. Without saying a word, he grasped hold of the handle of the shovel and exited the house. Outside, it was bitter as always. He carefully closed the front door behind him and leaning on the shovel, rested for a moment and observed the morning in front of him. The decorations on the tree were very few this year. Lothar himself had helped to erect the tree and a few of the villagers had painted ornaments for it. Half-painted, they hung languidly from the branches, watching the scene below them.

Very few people were out. Lothar could only see old Emma from a few houses north as she joylessly stumbled her way through the snow, likely heading for the graveyard to place the red flowers she held at the foot of her son's headstone. Spotting Lothar in the distance, she simply reclined her head in a short motion before continuing on her way.

A merry Christmas to you, Lothar thought. *If such a thing as merriment or joy still lingers. Perhaps somewhere among the stars.*

He looked upwards, as if in search for these stars, and his heart sank.

Oh no. Looks as though it's about to start snowing.

He sighed and then picked up the shovel. Before he could make a start on the snow, he heard footsteps. They were not the footsteps of Emma however, nor of anyone who might bring good fortune or cheer into his day. The steps sounded awfully like they belonged to someone with a limp. One step was much louder than the following, and they rang out in quick twos, much like the sound of a heartbeat.

THUMP *thump,* THUMP *thump,* THUMP *thump.*

Around the corner, a grey-haired man appeared. He wore peculiar trousers which had torn on one side, revealing a silver leg which shone against the white of the snow on the ground. Upon finding Lothar, the man began to shuffle slowly towards him.

'Hello Lars,' Lothar said. 'What news?'

'Since yesterday?' Lars questioned. 'Nothing. And if you ask me once again about your sister, so help me I'll climb the great mountain just to throw myself from the top if it.'

It had been well more than ten years since Lothar had seen Annika. She never wrote to him but he had heard much about her. From what Lothar understood, she had been well respected in the war for these past several years. She was known for her bravery; for running boldly into the very face of danger when most others would not. Once, he had heard, she had infiltrated an enemy camp single-handedly to rescue some children that had been taken hostage there. She'd almost been captured herself but had gotten away uninjured, save for a small scar on her right cheek which had apparently come from some awful spinning blade that had become common in the fighting. She'd disappeared completely some years previously, but Lothar had heard tell of a woman with a small scar spotted among the distant mountains fighting five enemy soldiers single-handedly before an avalanche had swept them all away.

'Would you like a hot drink?' Lothar asked. 'We've mostly run out of tea but could flavour the water with some herbs.'

'Aye,' Lars said. 'That would be grand.'

***

Lothar invited Lars into the house, but the old man insisted they palaver outside on one of the benches under the great Christmas tree instead. Taking their mugs with them, they cleared the snow from a bench and sat, wrapped warmly in fur coats and clinging to their mugs of weak but warm herbal tea.

'How's Yunie?' Lars asked.

'Quiet,' Lothar said. 'Barely a peep from her in the nights. It's funny, it's almost like she's so accustomed to this surrounding grief that she's learned to be a part of it. To sink into it unseen and hide among the sadness.'

Lars snorted. 'Don't we all do that?'

Lothar took a lugubrious sip from his mug. 'Not all of us. Some of us have tried to put a stop to it all.'

Lars looked round at Lothar beside him with an expression of hushed solace. 'Don't be angry with yourself. You're a father and a husband. Your place is here with Yunie and Freyja. And how *is* Freyja, by the way?'

Lothar sighed. 'She's as part of this gloom as anything else is. She goes through her day barely even looking at me, you know. It's like she's not only forgotten how to be happy, but she's forgotten what happiness is at all.'

'It may be that's the same for us all,' Lars said.

'Sometimes it feels like that,' Lothar began. 'But now and then I remember my childhood. *Early* childhood, that is. It's all fuzzy now, but I remember all of us being together. My family, I mean. I remember my mother's face was never seen without a smile set upon it. My father was the same. And Jonas and Annika were always so content and happy to play with me. Now they're all gone. My father is dead and my strongest memories of my sister are those of when she was just a child. She went to war at such a tender age. And then they all went, and I stayed.'

'For goodness' sake, Lothar, you can't be blamed. You stayed because you had a new family here that needed you.'

'And before that?' Lothar said, eyes fixed to the mug in front of him. 'I could have gone out to war then, only I didn't. I chose to stay. I'm a coward.'

'You were the last of your house,' Lars consoled. 'The village wouldn't have allowed it. You know that. Anyway, trust me, you wouldn't have wanted to be out there. It was awful.'

Was. Lothar hated how Lars would often talk of the war as though it was already over. Like grief had won and now anyone who had been left behind was just waiting for it to arrive completely like some ghoulish messenger and carry them off to a dismal, black oblivion.

'Who *are* they, Lars?' Lothar asked. 'The folk we're fighting?'

Lars looked up to the snow softly gliding from the sky. 'It's hard to say.'

'But you must know *something*,' Lothar persisted. 'You fought against them for years. Who are they? Where did they come from?'

Lars sighed and shook his head, solemnly. 'I'm not so sure they are what you'd call *folk,* Lothar.'

'What then?' Lothar asked. 'Animals? Creatures of some sort?'

'Not that either,' Lars said, staring off into the distance.

'What, then?'

Lars looked at Lothar now. 'Do you ever get a bad thought in your head? A foolish one, something small like you've forgotten to buy flour for the next day's bread? And then you forget all about it but that *feeling* still remains; the bad feeling. Only now that you've forgotten what caused that bad feeling in the first place it's gotten worse, because now your mind is sure that it's got to be something really awful. Something horrible is happening in your life, it's beyond your control and it's going to be really terrible for evermore. Then you remember it was just the flour, and you almost laugh because it was such a little thing. But somehow that feeling of pure dread remains, stuck to you like a fly stuck to a spider's web waiting for the inevitable. And suddenly every little anxiety in your life becomes this big, uncontrollable mess that's spiralling chaotically and causing all sorts of damage to all the other parts of your life. *That's* what we're fighting, Lothar. A feeling. One that should be within our control but isn't, and we don't know why. And I don't so much fear that it's winning anymore. I fear it's already won.'

***

'You left the shovel outside.'

Freyja's voice came blankly when Lothar arrived home later, closing the door quickly behind him to save what warmth was left in the house.

'Are you going to clear the path now?'

'Aye,' Lothar said. 'In a moment.'

Without taking his coat off or even glancing towards his wife and child, Lothar clambered up the stairs. Heading past the room that was his as a baby and the one he now shared with Freyja, he opened the door to the room that would be Yunie's when she was older. Walking inside, he closed the door behind him.

The room was cluttered with all sorts of bric-a-brac; old teapots and broken lanterns, spare pieces of wood and a collection of peculiar wind-up toys that had become more commonplace in the last few years. Cobwebs littered the walls and ceiling and dust puffed up from the floor. He made his way clumsily to the back of the room and put a few pieces of wood to the side in search of what he'd come in for. But before he found it, he came upon an old item that stopped him in his tracks.

A soft toy bobin. It was old now, and covered in dust. Its wide, unblinking eyes stared up at Lothar as though asking him why he hadn't come years sooner.

He picked up the toy and gently patted the dust from it. Poor thing. When had he last seen it?

Something stirred in his heart then. Some ancient and joyous connection from long ago that he shared with this bird. And now he could almost hear it sing but for the fact that it was lost. Here he held it in his hands, but somewhere in the ether the bobin's spirit had long vanished, never to return.

Oh, poor, poor thing.

He felt something on his cheek. A cold tear slid down his face.

Foolish! Weeping over a child's toy of old.

But that wasn't it. It wasn't the toy he was weeping for. It was the memories attached to it. The time when people felt happy. All gone. Vanished into the wind like the smoke of a fire lit by joy itself.

Gone, gone, gone.

And at this moment, he found it. The item he'd come in search of. He placed the bobin gently down and reaching for the long, metallic item in the corner, he picked it up and held it out in front of him, staring grimly at it.

Awful thing. But I suppose in these desperate times we must use it.

The rifle was light in his hands. Old thing, well used. It had been his father's once. Had he died with it in his hands? Best not to dwell on such thoughts.

The tear in his eye had been the last true sign; if he could feel so strongly about the memories of the past then there surely was still something in him that wanted to defeat the evil out there once and for all? His tear was not a weakness, it was a sign. A sign that the war was not over. Yes, it had been raging for years, yes, they still had no idea exactly *what* it was they were fighting and yes, many had died trying. But the enemy was yet to face Lothar. Oh, how they would tremble when they saw him!

But to leave Freyja and Yunie? Could he really do that? His mother and father had left him, after all. Because sometimes a thing would come along that was too important. Sometimes a great corruption engulfed everything that anyone had ever loved. And at times like these, fathers would leave daughters, mothers would leave sons. But it was for the benefit of all. It had to happen.

But Yunie is so young! Barely out of the womb!

And even as he thought of her, Lothar could hear his daughter cry from downstairs.

Freyja will attend to her.

But she didn't. Yunie's cries came harder and more desperately. What was going on?

'Freyja!' Lothar shouted down. 'Freyja, Yunie is crying! Why aren't you going to her?'

Nothing.

A sudden panic took over in Lothar. He put the gun down and made for the door.

'Freyja?'

Yunie was screaming now. Crying with all the might that her little lungs could muster. Lothar reached the stairs and could see her in her rocking basket. Her face was red, mouth wide open and eyes scrunched up as she continued to wail. Where was Freyja?

'Freyja!' Lothar called again. His heart was now beating rapidly against his chest.

He went to Yunie and picked her up, held her close to his shoulder and patted her softly on the back.

'There there, little one. It's okay. Your father is here.'

But where is your mother?
On the table. A note.

Keeping hold of Yunie in one arm, he picked up the piece of parchment from the table, and his eyes widened as he read.

Lothar,

    I cannot continue to burden you or Yunie. I am not myself. I don't expect I shall see you again.

    I'm sorry.

Freyja

No, no no!!

He raced to the door, squeezing Yunie in his arms as she continued to sob. The cries escaped her more fervently now, as though she knew what Lothar knew; her mother had gone with every intention of staying away and never returning. Gone, just like Jonas and Annika, like Malin and Sander. The only difference was that she hadn't gone to war. She had no doubt gone looking for death in its quietest and most unhappy place.

Lothar flung the front door open widely and stepped outside. It was lightly snowing now and the dark skies cast an ominous shadow over the village.

'Freyja!!' Lothar bellowed into the air. *'Freyja!!'*

He hadn't expected a response of any kind, yet the expected silence still hurt him. Yunie wailed, joining her father's shouts for her mother. Together, the pair of them bellowed into the empty village with its bare trees and snowed-over homes. Distant, tremulous echoes were the only response.

'Freeeeeeyyyyyjaaaaa!!'

Lothar let his voice trail off at the end of his final shout before sinking to his knees in the snow, holding his baby daughter close to him and openly weeping.

***

Yunie had taken a long time to settle. Lothar had lit the fireplace and sat with her, talking to her and gently rocking her. But nothing would calm her; she wanted her mother's touch, she missed her mother's smell. But finally, she had quietened and stared at her father with wide, loving and yet still so saddened eyes.

'It's okay, my love,' Lothar had said. 'Daddy is here. I will never leave you, my little beauty. I will be here, always.'

But even as he had said the words, he remembered how easily the misery had taken Freyja. He remembered how she had once beamed with joy. Yet even she had succumbed to the same poison that the rest of the world apparently had. Would he yield to the same thing?

He couldn't. He couldn't leave little Yunie.

Except, you were going to tonight. Freyja simply got there before you.

Presently he lay Yunie down in the cot of the room that had once been his own, a very long time ago. Her little eyes watered once more and she began some gurgling sniffles.

'Wait, wait my love…'

He exited the room briefly and returned with something in hand, which he placed in the cot next to Yunie. The old bobin toy. She looked at it and it seemed to work that same old magic which had once resonated with Lothar. The sniffles stopped in an instant and she looked at the bird calmly, with a childish wonder in her tiny blue eyes.

'There you are,' Lothar said softly. 'Yes, she has that effect on people, that little bird. She was mine once. You can have her now. Merry Christmas, little one.'

It was her only gift; neither Lothar nor Freyja had gotten anything for their daughter's first Christmas. They hadn't exchanged gifts with anyone. But at least there in that room, the spirit of that ancient tradition remained intact but for that one special moment.

Yunie's eyes were closing now.

'Yes, sleep,' Lothar whispered. 'Sleep and dream of wonderful things. For in our dreams we may live our most joyfully and see all those secret, happy things we oft miss with our eyes fully opened. Sleep, my daughter.'

Her eyelids closed and Lothar bent down to kiss her on the forehead. When he was sure that she was sleeping he walked quietly to the window of her room where he could see much of the village. Not a soul was to be seen as the falling snowflakes began to bury the shovel by the front door.

4
Silent Night, Woeful Night

Joy was frozen to the bone.

She painfully picked herself up. Her arms and legs were aching. Even the cold air she breathed in felt agonising. How long had she been lying underneath the tree and watching Lothar's memory?

Stupid. Shouldn't have allowed myself to linger here. Time's running out.

Running out for what? She was forgetting something. Lothar's memories seemed now to mix with her own. She'd witnessed the abandonment of the village to the point where it resembled the very same place that Joy had seen and felt in the real world.

And then the image of the huge, black wolf sprung back into her mind.

Hunter. The thing called itself Hunter.

Despicable thing. Wretched thing. What was its plan? It caught a scent. A scent of someone succumbing to the sadness...

How I love to feed from the youth. Especially children.

Joy began pacing around now. The deep-rooted depression that had started to take hold of her suddenly quelled at the thought of the wolf. It was after someone. Someone else still alive in this place. Likely that it was Lothar, the only person other than herself that she knew had gone up this mountain.

She looked up towards the great slope ahead of her and could see no sign of a light. But then, hadn't she left the lantern she'd been carrying? The moons above had given off enough light to go by when the clouds had cleared, and now several thousands of glittering stars had joined them, beaming their light sadly below to light up the snow of the mountain in a pale radiance.

Got to move forwards. Got to find Lothar.

'Fortune!' Joy called out into the darkness. 'Fortune! Where are you?'

At the sound of her name, the bobin loyally floated into Joy's view and perched in her favourite position on her shoulder.

'Come on, my friend,' Joy whispered. 'We've got to move.'

***

Gasping and panting for air, Joy willed herself onwards and up the great ascent of the mountain. She saw no footprints in the snow as she went, but didn't think much of it; although it had stopped now, the snowfall in the last few hours had been enough to cover Lothar's tracks had he gone up here several hours before. But what about the wolf? It had bounded up the mountain as soon as it had caught the scent, and this certainly wasn't hours ago.

Or was it? How long had Joy been in the trance-like state she always entered when witnessing the reflection of old memories? She'd often wondered this; sometimes she would find an old memory that lasted an entire day, such as Lothar's, and yet she would awaken and it would seem as though the time in her reality hadn't moved. Other times she would be sure that the world had passed her by while she had slept and watched a memory of a brief walk from one end of a street to another. Who was to say that she hadn't now been here on this planet for many days?

She shuddered. *Don't think about that. Just keep going. Forwards, always.*

The incline became steeper yet and Joy was frustrated to be moving slower, wasting time in trudging up the same path that Hunter would have easily breezed past before her. Her body shook with the extra exertion of it, and Fortune flew from her shoulder, choosing to once again fly ahead a little and then wait.

'Of course, you'll never have this problem, will you?' Joy said to the bobin. 'I've never wished I could fly as much as I do now. Maybe you can go on ahead and let me know what you see up there?'

Joy wasn't surprised when the bird gave a small chirp and then swiftly flew upwards towards one of the great moons in the sky. This one was the closest and looked very large. It was almost like another planet hanging in the sky, its blue-grey light beaming down onto the mountain. She almost wanted to stop and admire it for a while, but she allowed herself only the briefest of pauses before continuing her difficult climb upwards.

Her feet were frigid; much of the snow had managed to get inside her boots and had wetted her socks which now clung to her like icy cloths. The cold seemed to travel all the way up her calves to her knees, which ached with the chill. This made the effort of climbing all the more laborious.

But what's the point in climbing? You'll find nothing up there. Nothing but –

Perhaps a building of some sort. Somewhere she could be indoors. Maybe even build a fire. She could rest up a little and make sure she was warm before continuing.

Don't be stupid. You'll never be warm again. You'll die of the cold up here. There's no protection against –

And even if there was no building there might perhaps be a cave. A dry one at that.

With a large black wolf waiting to pounce on you. Waiting to –

'Stop it,' she said aloud, calmly.

And at least for the moment, it stopped.

***

Not much further up the mountain, Joy found the strangest thing.

She hadn't seen it until she'd accidentally kicked it, stumbled and fallen over into a puff of snow. It had made a metallic sound. Picking herself up, she retraced her steps and found what looked to be a long piece of metal.

A gun? One of the rifles she'd seen Lothar and Jonas handle?

She tried to pick it up but it wouldn't budge. It seemed as though it was somehow trapped underneath the snow. She brushed as much snow away as she could find, and then recoiled in shock when she found another part of the metal object attached at the end and looking very familiar.

A hand. A metal hand attached to what must have been a metal arm. She was reminded instantly of Lars, from Lothar's last memory. He had limped on what looked to be a silver leg. Presumably he had lost his real leg in the war and had had it replaced with a metal one. It was odd, come to think of it; Joy hadn't seen many metallic items on this planet. It seemed that they hadn't reached that stage of development yet. If those in the observation department had been interested, they'd have classed this planet under category D – developing technology but still very primal in many areas.

Yet here appeared to be an intricately designed arm and hand. The fingers had metal fingernails, and even slight wrinkles at the knuckles. The arm was plain enough but designed and shaped in the way that it looked to belong to a relatively fit and muscular person. Joy began to wonder just how finely detailed Lars' leg had been.

But that didn't appear to be all. At the shoulder of the arm, buried under the snow, appeared to be an entire *body*.

Joy felt a little anxious at first, but decided that she needed to uncover the rest of this thing. Picking up large clumps of snow and shovelling them to the side, she began to uncover all that was underneath. Piece by piece and bit by bit, she indeed revealed a whole… person. Made entirely of metal.

It's like a… a robot…
It can't be!

It was lying face down in the snow, its left arm, the one Joy had first discovered, out to its side as though it had tried to break a fall. She could see no signs of damage anywhere.

In its right hand, still partially buried, it held a rifle.

Joy carefully picked it up and inspected it. It looked exactly like the one Lothar had held in the moments before discovering Freyja had left. Having no experience in any kind of firearms, Joy felt uncomfortable holding the gun, and had no way of knowing whether it was at all safe to do so.

Except, my Sense could probably help that…

She felt a small urge to take the gun with her. Use it if she had to. She had no idea what other grim mysteries this mountain held, but she did know at least that there was a great black wolf up here somewhere, and that a rifle might be just the thing to keep it at bay.

But no. No, no, no. Something felt altogether wrong about the idea of taking it. She carefully lowered it back into the snow, muzzle pointing downwards, and let go of it. Standing above the frame of the metal body, she stared down at it. Should she try to move it to get a look at the face? Maybe it was far better not to – Joy had no way of knowing whether it was really dead, and maybe it would see her and instantly consider her an enemy. The people of this planet were what Joy would call human, much like herself. Chances were, it would see her and think of her as belonging to the village or a nearby town. Best just to leave it where it lay.

Turning from it, she continued up the slope of the mountain. Her legs still ached, and she now had no feeling at all in her toes. Her face had become hard and stinging. She thought her cheeks were probably as red as Fortune's breast, and allowed herself the smallest of giggles at the thought that she might have discovered why all bobins have those red chests.

There, you see! If you can still laugh, there's still hope.

Hope...

A sudden surge of guilt wrapped around Joy. She had barely thought about her sister since the last attempt at calling. Fumbling inside her pocket now she picked up the radio and saw to her prompt glee that it had picked up a strong signal. She let air rush out of her frozen lips and watched it steam the screen of the radio. Her fingers were so numb from the cold she found it almost impossible to press the right buttons to call her sister. After what seemed like an endless amount of attempts, she successfully started calling.

Hope answered almost instantly.

'Hello? Joy?' Hope's voice was weak, sleepy, detached.

'Hope!' Joy called. 'Yeah, it's me! It's Joy!'

Her sister's reply was like an icy stab through the heart.

'Oh. Hi.'

And then silence. Joy didn't know what to say, and thought that even if she had the words, the sounds from her mouth would be difficult to produce; her little sister's reaction to the call was like hearing that a loved one had passed away.

She pretty much has now, anyway though, hasn't she? She's as good as gone. She'd probably be eaten already if that wolf had been there instead of on –

'Hope,' Joy interrupted. 'Are you okay?'

A short pause, followed by, 'Okay? What do you mean, okay?'

'You sound...' Joy began.

Sad? Of course she's sad. Everyone in the universe is sad. Distant is probably a better word to describe it. As though she's trying to distance herself from you because she knows her time is nearly –

'Hope,' Joy interrupted again. 'It's going to be okay. Everything will be alright.'

'What?' Hope asked, sounding genuinely baffled.

'You're going to smile again,' Joy said, and she even smiled herself as if trying to prove it was possible. 'You're going to be happy again, Hope. Very soon.'

'No,' Hope answered quietly. 'No, I don't think I will.'

'*Of course* you will!' Joy said, as brightly as she could.

No, she won't. Stop lying to your sister. She'll be sad for the rest of her short life. She'll be miserable and lonely and –

'Listen to me,' Joy said. 'Do you remember that story you used to love? The one about the mouse?'

There was silence on the other end of the radio. All Joy could hear now was the gentle wind whistling past the mountain on its way to greet the stars.

Eventually, Hope spoke again. 'Suree,' she said.

'Yes!' Joy said. 'Suree the mouse who lived on the third moon!'

'That's a children's story,' Hope said. 'I always loved it when you told it.'

'Stories are everything we are, Hope.'

There was a pause again. Joy looked to the stars now, and for the first time since arriving on this planet, wondered which of them shone down on her own planet. Even among those that looked closest, she knew her little sister was still light years away. She suddenly felt so far away and so very small. Like a tiny mouse that lived on a vast, faraway moon.

'Would you like me to tell you the story again?' Joy asked.

'The story of Suree?' Hope asked. She sounded astonished.

'Yeah,' Joy smiled, hoping her sister could hear it. 'Why not? It's one of my favourite stories. At times like these, a good story might be all we need.'

'Yeah,' Hope said after another moment's pause. 'Yeah, I would love that.'

Joy waded through the snow and found a large rock jutting out from the ground. She cleared much of the snow from it and sat on the cold stone. She looked up at the twinkling stars once more, drew in a deep, cold breath, and began the tale.

'Long ago,' she said. 'There was a mouse called Suree…'

And she recounted the entire story. The lonely mouse who lived on the third moon and the little girl who gazed up to it every night, wishing with all her heart to visit poor old Suree. The mighty bird, which traditionally had been something like an eagle, but Joy changed on this occasion to a bobin, who would allow the girl to ride on its great back all the way to the moon.

'What's a bobin?' Hope asked.

'One of those little birds with the red chest and the yellow beak,' Joy replied.

'It's too little for a girl to ride on,' Hope said.

'No,' Joy assured. 'This one is a *giant* bobin. And the friendliest in all the universe.'

'What's its name?' Hope asked.

'Fortune,' Joy said. 'She's called Fortune.'

And she continued with the tale. Of how the little girl arrived on the moon and was delighted to have met the mouse, who had turned out to be very friendly, but so very lonely. Of the various adventures of the girl and the mouse as they played together and joyfully slid down the craters. Of how the little girl became sad when her time to leave had arrived, and how Suree wept with all her heart to lose her new best friend. And oh, so suddenly! And then how the bobin named Fortune promised to fly the little girl back to the moon any time she wanted – each and every night if she so wished. And how the mouse and the girl's hearts had been filled with the purest form of happiness.

'And the girl fell asleep on the back of the bobin as she carried her all the way back home. Fortune tucked her into bed where she dreamed of flying. And the next morning, she awoke with delight and love in her heart, and was ready to share it all with everyone she passed.'

When Joy finished the tale, silence once more fell between the pair. Joy wondered if perhaps the signal had been cut again but she didn't want to look.

Not now. She'd rather take in this moment of peace. This here and now, where she didn't feel completely abysmally sad, so lost in the sheer glum that had so blanketed reality.

Eventually, Hope's failing voice came through.

'Joy... What's happened to the spaceship?'

Now Joy did look at the screen on the radio. Strong signal. Sixty-four per cent battery. No getting out of it this time. And what was more, the screen was now filled with the live image of her little sister, many light years away. She looked so, so very sad. She wasn't looking into her own radio; her eyes were still and fixed onto a point on the faraway wall. There was no colour in her face, and Joy was instantly reminded of the child's drawings from earlier. How they had once been so full of colour. And how they had become so frightfully devoid of it.

Yes, yes! Tell her! Tell your little sister that you won't be seeing her again! Tell her that whatever life awaits you will be without her! Tell her –

'Oh, Hope...' Joy began. 'Hope, please don't be sad, or angry at me...'

'It's broken, isn't it?' Hope said, distantly.

'Please try to understand...' Joy said.

Understand? Understand! You've left her alone! Just like your parents left you alone. Just like Lothar's parents left him alone. Just like Lothar will have left Yunie alone. You didn't even think about her, did you? Where is she now? Probably –

'I understand,' Hope said. 'You're not coming back.' Her voice was failing even more now. It sounded hopeless.

'I want to!' Joy said. 'I really do! Of course I do! I crashed and...'

It's your fault, you foolish girl! Your fault! Your –

'I'm going to hang up now,' Hope said.

Your fault! Your fault! Your fault! Your fault! Your –

'No! Hope, please! Just wait!'

Your fault! Your fault! Your fault! Your fault! Your fault! Your fault! Your fault! Your fault! Your fault! Your fault! Your –

'SHUT UP!!!'

Overcome by sheer fury, Joy stood up and hurtled the radio away. It smacked hard against another rock and she saw pieces of it fly and tumble down the mountainside.

'Oh! What have I done!?'

She ran after the radio and found the biggest piece of it. The screen was cracked, the battery was missing, and it wouldn't turn on.

And I'm still here, Joy.
I'm always here.

***

There was nothing to do but plunge onwards. She had discarded the broken piece of radio, left it in the snow by the rock she had smashed it against. She let her heavy legs carry her more slowly as she walked, head sloped downwards, staring at the white snow crunching underneath her boots as she went.

Her face was filled with bitter, cold tears. She would never speak to her sister again. Her little sister, who sounded like she had given up hope to the point where she might not even go by the name of it anymore. What was she doing now? Joy imagined a darkened and cold room, where Hope sat alone and simply stared into the blackness. She would sit there now until it was time to die in the same way that Eric had. Only, there was nobody there to hold her hand as she faded away.

Onwards. Upwards. Step by step and tear by tear, pushing and climbing, willing herself onwards not because she had any sense of aspiration left, but because it was the only thing left to her other than sitting down and accepting death here on this mountain of an alien planet where the only thing colder than the snow was the irreparably broken spirit.

And then she heard it. The very last semblance of the rumour known as hope. The tweeting of a bobin.

Fortune appeared in front of her, chirping wildly. She fluttered down to the ground in front of her and began jumping up and down and moving her yellow beak upwards to the top of a cliff. Joy could reach it via a steep slope to the side of it if she was very careful.

'Very well, Fortune,' she said. 'One last adventure won't kill anyone. What's up there, anyway?'

The bird continued chirping madly, and then fluttered to Joy's shoulder as she began her scramble up the steep slope to the side of the cliff.

She hadn't gotten far up when she once again kicked the metal frame of one of the robotic people.

'Here, too?' she said aloud. 'Who are you people?'

As she climbed up the slope, she had to lean forwards and use her hands as well as her feet to ascend, and she placed a hand on a metallic leg here, a silver arm there. There appeared to be hundreds of them here. All dead, unmoving.

And then she found the other bodies scattered among them.

Humans. People who looked just like the ones she'd seen in Lothar's memories. They lay here among the metal people with their eyes closed. Killed in battle no doubt, yet they looked entirely peaceful. They barely looked as though they'd been in any kind of fight at all. If Joy didn't know better, she might have easily convinced herself that she was having a strange dream about climbing a mountain and weaving in between several sleeping men and women.

And she felt oddly removed from the situation. As though these people *were* indeed simply asleep. She felt no sadness about it. Nothing at all.

But she quickly realised that this was only because she had already been overcome with grief. Nothing else could add to it anymore. She'd reached the climax of what one could feel within the realms of sadness and depression. What was one more dead body? A hundred more? Who cares about another miniscule fading star in an entire universe of dying worlds beyond worlds? A final farewell from the very last spark of happiness?

And barely noticing, she reached the top of the slope. To her side, the great cliff jutted out from the mountain, and Joy witnessed a scene that somehow injected a fresh dose of urgency into her heart.

She had come upon a small wooden cabin, situated just at the top of the cliff. Through a small window, she could see that a dim fire was burning. Someone had been here. But it wasn't this that had awoken her urgency; just beyond the cabin, she saw something else. The great black wolf. Hunter. Its teeth were bared and it looked to be stalking something. Disgusting amounts of sticky saliva poured out of its greedy mouth as it eyed a small thing on the floor some distance off.

Joy's Sense went into overdrive. It told her to make not for the wolf, but for the cabin. Just to the side of it was a leafless tree, and she instinctively snapped a thick branch from it before bursting into the cabin.

The fireplace.

The fire here was nearly out. The last crackles were sounding out and the warm glow was fading. In the room there was a table with various scattered materials. She quickly grabbed a piece of cloth and wrapped it tightly around the branch, tying it with smaller, thinner pieces.

It'll have to do. Go! *Go!*

A bottle. She didn't need to sniff it to know that it was alcohol of some kind. She poured it greedily onto the cloth, threw the bottle to the side and lit her torch with the last flames of the fireplace. She dashed outside.

Hunter was closer to its prey now. It was grinning. Joy sprinted forwards.

'Hey!!' she bellowed. 'Hey, you!! *Wolf!!*'

Hunter looked up at her, and its face instantly changed to a hard scowl.

Continuing to dart through the snow, torch in hand, Joy could now see exactly what it was the wolf had been stalking.

A little girl. No older than seven or eight. She sat in the snow hugging her knees, not looking at Joy and not looking at the wolf. She merely sat with a look on her face that was devoid of anything hopeful or joyous.

How I love to feed from the youth. Especially children.

'No!!' Joy shouted. 'You stay away from her! *You stay away from her, Wolf!!'*

Reaching the child, Joy flung herself in between her and Hunter, holding the torch out towards the wolf warningly.

'Foolish girl!' Hunter jeered. 'What do you think you can do to stop me feasting on this child?'

Joy looked the wolf dead in its eyes.

'Everything I can,' she said.

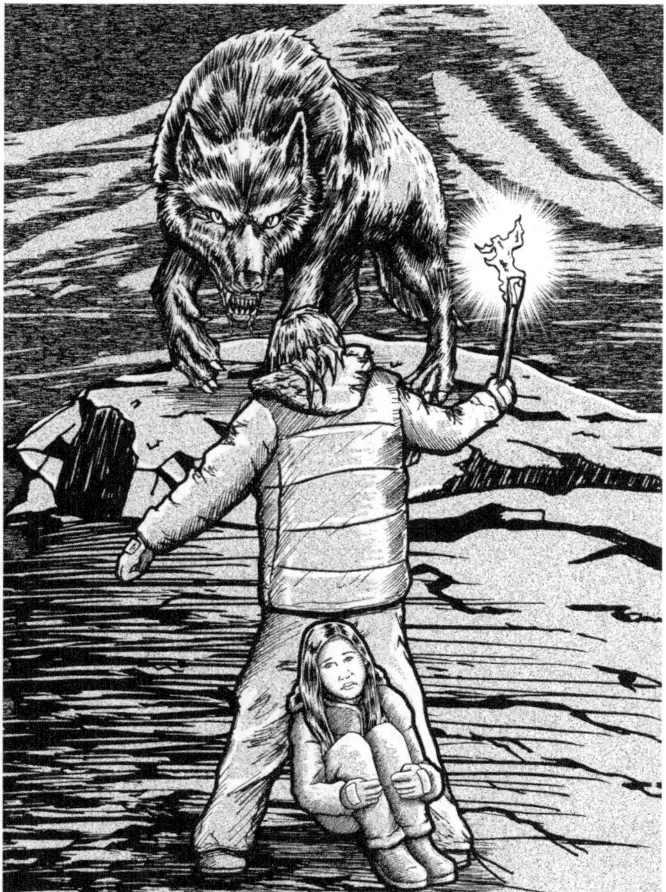

Hunter threw its head back and howled a laugh so vile that Joy felt disgust rise up inside her. She didn't dare to look back behind her to see the reaction of the child, but she wasn't afraid that the girl herself may have been terrified; she feared that even this shrill, evil replacement noise for what was supposed to be laughter may not have removed the empty look from her face.

'What are you going to do, Woman?' the wolf hissed. 'You are no warrior. Plenty have tried to kill me and all have failed.'

'You will not touch this child!' Joy insisted. 'I'd give my own life to protect her!'

'You may yet,' Hunter smiled. 'There's a strong scent about you. You're fading. You will taste good.'

'And what will you do when there's nobody left, Wolf?' Joy said. She held the torch closer still towards Hunter, and for a fleeting moment, she could have sworn that the wolf had backed off a step.

'Oh, dear young thing,' Hunter cooed. 'You really have no idea of what I am, do you? When there's nobody left in this world I shall move on to the next. The universe is full of misery.'

Misery... Hadn't she named the wolf such on her first meeting with it?

'No...' Joy breathed aloud.

Hunter grunted. 'What's that? What are you saying, woman?'

'My name is not *Woman*,' Joy retorted. 'My name is *Joy*. And I said no. Your name is not Misery.'

'My name is...' started the wolf.

'Woe,' Joy said. 'I name you Woe. Because all that is woeful deserves pity, and I pity you deepest of all. Skulking around looking to feed from those less fortunate than yourself, a miserable, piteous, pathetic creature that hides in the shadows.'

The wolf's face twisted into a scowl so fierce it might have knocked braver people off their feet with just a single glance. It said nothing, but a low growl started from deep within its chest. Joy took a step forwards. The wolf took a step back.

'What can be more utterly wretched than an animal that takes delight in finding children who have lost everything that made them shine?' Joy said. 'I pity you, Woe, I really do. I feel sorry for you.'

'You will call me *Hunter!*' the wolf snarled. Its sharp teeth showed menacingly in the light from Joy's torch.

'No,' Joy said, calmly. 'I will not.'

'Then you will die a foolish oaf who should have known true power when she saw it!' Woe said, but did not move.

Joy stood where she was, as still as the mountain itself. 'Come on then. What are you waiting for? Come and get me.'

Woe began its deep rumbling growl once more, but still did not move.

'What's the matter?' Joy asked. 'I'm standing right here with no gun. I imagine those you brag about defeating all had one, didn't they? Maybe a few of them even shot you, but it had no effect? Well here I stand, Woe the wolf, with no weapon of any sort... Just this torch.'

The wolf's growl became louder.

'Ah, but that's just it, isn't it?' Joy said. 'The torch. You fear it. The big bad wolf is afraid of fire. This fire. The one made from hope.'

'Curse you!' Woe said. Its voice becoming quieter. 'But no matter – you and that child both are fading. It's simply a matter of time. You'll reach the end. And when you do, I'll be there to greet you.'

And saying no more, the wolf turned and once again disappeared into the darkness and the mountain behind it.

***

Joy bent down and wrapped an arm around the child. She was deathly cold.

'Come on,' Joy said. 'You can't stay here. You need to get warm.'

Using her free, torch-less hand, she took the child's hand and pulled. The girl made no move to stand.

'Come on,' Joy said again. 'It's okay. I'm here to help.'

Still, the child wouldn't move.

Please! Joy thought. *Please stand, little girl! You'll die if you stay here. Please!*

She didn't want to hurt the girl. Remembering how her own body had begun to ache with the cold, she knew it might take the smallest of tugs in the wrong way to inflict pain on her. She was wearing a coat and gloves, but this wouldn't have been close to enough halfway up the great mountain of a frozen planet.

Eventually, Joy was able to get the child to her feet and found that she was led with relative ease towards the cabin, where the light was even dimmer than it had been when she had first arrived. She made sure to shut the door firmly behind her and then attended to the fire. She was able to re-stoke the flames quickly, and the room filled with radiant warmth.

'There,' Joy said. 'Isn't that better?'

The child still didn't speak, and her face held that same lack of happiness that had been present before.

With the room now lit in a warm light, Joy found that there was a bed in here. She led the child to it and lay her down, wrapping the blankets snugly around here. As she did so, she felt the girl shiver slightly.

'There we are,' Joy said. 'Don't you feel better? That fire should blaze for a good few hours now.'

Kneeling at her bedside, Joy looked tenderly at the child's blue face. Her eyes were wide open, staring at Joy as if she wanted to ask who she was, where she came from, and why in the cold world she had cared so much for her wellbeing.

She looked so much like her father.

'Your name is Yunie, isn't it?' Joy said. 'It's a beautiful name.'

Still, the girl said nothing.

'You don't feel like talking?' Joy asked. 'That's okay. Let's just get you rested and warm.'

But then something happened that took Joy aback. Yunie did speak. But the words came heart wrenchingly unexpected.

'Are you going to leave me?'

Joy wiped at her face to chase away the tear before it had the chance to appear. 'No,' she said. 'No, I'm not. I'll stay awhile.'

Looking across the room to the table where she'd found the pieces of fabric, Joy spotted a chair. She slid it over to Yunie's bedside and sat there, calmed by the glow from the fire.

Yes. Yes, stay awhile.

She closed her eyes.

Stay awhile, Joy. Stay. This place is, of course, full of strong memory...

~

When Yunie awoke, she didn't know what it was o'clock. This wasn't unusual; the days were always so dark because the sky was filled by a giant snow cloud that seemed to refuse to burst. She looked to her window, which told the same tale as it always did: it hadn't started to snow yet, but outside it was still as cold and empty as it ever was.

She lay still, breathing lightly as she stared out of the window. On the windowsill sat an old stuffed toy bobin. Her father had told her it had used to be his, once upon a time. He said that it had had some strange ability to bring joy to both of them. He never understood it, he said, but whatever kind of mysterious magic the old toy had once possessed was gone. It sat at the window, dusty, cold and worn, staring out at an entire world that seemed to have lost its old spark of yore.

She sat up now and slowly stretched. Yawning, she slid on her slippers and walked over to the window, looking out at the empty scene with her friend, the bobin. It was the same as always; empty houses and snow-covered paths with no footprints. The great tree with its odd ornaments stood in the middle and sighed to wake once more to find its home deserted. Yunie often wondered if she and her father might have been the very last people left in the village. If it weren't for the occasional visit from one of her father's old friends or a quiet passing in the street with fellow humans, she would have completely believed it. Life was quiet. Quiet and mournful.

Presently, she smelled something pleasant. Had Father had been cooking? Her stomach rumbled at the thought and she made for her door. Coming down the stairs, the smell grew stronger and she could hear her father softly signing a strange song.

And the soul felt its worth
A thrill of hope
The weary world rejoices
For yonder breaks
A new and glorious morn

Something about the song made Yunie feel strange. Although it was completely unfamiliar to her, she couldn't help but feel an attachment of some sort to it. Coming down the last step, she saw her father busy at the stove preparing food. Smoke billowed out of pots as he cheerfully swept around them, stirring and giving an occasional soft shake. He spotted her a moment later and smiled broadly.

'Yunie, my love! Good morning!'

Lothar's face, although only some seven or eight years older since he had found Freyja's note and lost her, was aged. Lines of sadness covered a bearded face with eyes that took pity on themselves. But they also radiated warmth and affection as they set upon Yunie.

'What were you singing?' Yunie asked.

Lothar's face remained much the same; almost devoid of joy, but not of hope. Not yet.

'It's an old song,' he said. 'A carol.'

Yunie walked over to the kitchen table and took a seat. 'What's a carol?'

Lothar sat opposite his daughter and continued to smile. 'Oh, this place used to be full of them at this time of year. Especially today. You'd hear singing all through the day and deep into the night.'

'What's so special about this time of year?'

Yunie could see her father's heart beginning to sink slightly at this, but the warmth in his face still resolutely clung on.

'My dearest daughter,' Lothar said. 'What a terrible father I have been through your tender years.'

Yunie said and felt little from these words. Having had but a paltry amount of experiences with people other than her father, she hadn't much of an idea of what was expected or considered good about a parent, or even a friend. He was nice to her, he looked after her, and on two or three occasions he had made her laugh. He seemed fine to her.

'All your young years,' Lothar continued. 'I have never celebrated Christmas with you.'

'Christmas?' Yunie repeated, saying the word for the very first time.

'Yes…' Lothar's voice trailed off, and for the first time this morning his smile faded somewhat from his face. 'Christmas, Yunie. It used to be the best time of the year.'

The best time of the year? Yunie thought. *What was so special about it? Why did it stop? What exactly was it?*

Lothar continued, 'The whole village would wake up with a sparkle in their eyes. It always snowed, and the children would ride their sledges down the great hill.'

Yunie was confused at this. 'The hill where Grandfather is buried?'

Something about what she had said seemed to bring a further dismay to Lothar's face. 'Yes. It wasn't always like that though, my love. I remember when that graveyard didn't exist at all.'

'Was that a long time ago?' Yunie asked.

'Longer now than it seems,' Lothar said, distantly. 'The entire village would exchange gifts, and often stay awhile, looking out for each other. Enjoying one another's company. Those were the days.'

Yunie paused in thought at what her father was saying for a moment, before sniffing the air and noticing just how hungry she was.

'What are you cooking?' she asked.

'Ah!' Lothar's smile returned, and he turned his attention back to the steaming pots on the stove. He'd already prepared two bowls at the side of it and now scooped the contents of the pots into them before taking them to the table.

'What is it?' Yunie asked, curiously.

'There is no name for it, I think,' Lothar said. 'A creation of my own.'

Inside the bowl was what looked like scrambled eggs and fish. It was a peculiar combination but it smelled wonderful, and Yunie began to eat hungrily.

'Do you like it?' Lothar asked.

Yunie nodded enthusiastically. It brought a keener smile yet to the face of her father.

'So...' Yunie said after swallowing some fish. 'Did *everybody* take part in Chris...'

'Christmas?' Lothar finished for her. 'Yes, everyone in this village and all the towns and villages beyond.'

Yunie thought about this and then asked the question that she'd been pondering ever since her father had started talking about this Christmas thing.

'Why?'

'*Why?*' Lothar repeated, confusedly. 'Well... because...'

'I mean, how did it start?' Yunie asked.

Her father had stopped eating his own breakfast and was now staring at the ceiling as though it somehow concealed the answer to his daughter's question.

'I suppose,' Lothar started. 'I suppose nobody knows. Or if they once did, they don't anymore. But it was never about that, Yunie. It was never about who started it and why it was thought up in the first place.'

'What was it about, Father?' Yunie asked.

'Joy,' Lothar answered immediately. 'Joy and love. Friendship and family. Happiness. A time of the year where all men and women saw each other as equals. Fellow passengers to the... to the... well, never mind where.'

But Yunie knew. More than this, she knew that *her father knew* that she knew. He was talking, grimly, of that mournful place in the village where he had once sledged as a boy, and was now filled with the headstones of those who had fought and died in some old, terrible war. A war that neither Yunie nor her father knew for certain had ever ended. What *had* they fought and died for? Were they living in a dismal yet quiet peace that had only been brought about by the sacrifice of those people beyond the stone wall and iron gates? And if they had lost, what would the village look like now? Might Yunie and her father have died?

Lothar rose from the table, his breakfast unfinished. Walking to the fireplace, he stoked the dying flames there and soon had a fresh fire blazing. When he turned around to face his daughter again, it was with another smile.

'Shall we go for a walk?' he asked.

***

Walking around the village was always difficult. The snow was deep and no paths had been cleared for many years. Lothar had told Yunie once that a walk around the entire village would have taken only twenty or so minutes in days gone by. Now it took an hour, even more if you stumbled often and had to keep picking yourself up.

It was cold, as always, but Yunie was wrapped up in her fur coat, hat, scarf and warm gloves. All of these clothes had once belonged to an aunt she had never met named Annika.

She never knew you, Lothar had said. *But she would be thrilled to pass on these clothes to you.*

Yunie never engaged much in conversation about Aunt Annika or Uncle Jonas. It seemed to cause her father a substantial amount of pain to talk about them, and she decided that it would be better to save him the torment. They had once all lived together in the same house. The very same that was now only hers and her father's. She wondered sometimes what it might have been like – how different the house might have looked and how different if might have *felt*. What exactly was joy? She'd heard her father talk of it before, but she had failed to understand it. Some grown-up concept she needn't worry about now. Maybe when she was older she would understand.

They trudged, father and daughter, through the thick snow and around the side of the great tree. Lothar held his daughter's hand as they went.

'That tree isn't supposed to always be there,' Lothar said. 'It's supposed to only be up at Christmas time.'

'Why?' Yunie asked.

Lothar chuckled a little. 'It's supposed to be special. When I was a boy, the sightings of the first Christmas trees in the village were an exciting thing. It meant that it was nearly time.'

'Who put this one up?' Yunie asked. 'And why didn't they take it back down after Christmas?'

Lothar looked at the tree with a sort of lost fondness. 'I helped put it up. Alongside Hannes and

Gunnar. And Eric, too. I wonder how Eric is... we should perhaps visit him soon. He hasn't been himself.'

Lothar looked to a house where Yunie could see that a dim fire was lit. She knew who Eric was, but knew very little about him. One of her father's old friends, from the days of joy no doubt.

They made it to an area of the village where the houses were more widely spread apart.

'We'd sometimes have a market here at Christmas,' Lothar said. 'If folk from the other settlements wanted to come over. It didn't happen very often. I can only remember it once in my youth. It was always cheery though.'

'Cheery?' Yunie said. 'That sounds like the word *cheer*.'

'Yes...' Lothar said, distantly. 'Yes, it does.'

Yunie thought she might understand a little of what her father had meant by joy now. But it was still difficult to fully comprehend. It wasn't simply that she hadn't ever experienced this thing, it was more that she hadn't felt much of *anything* before. Often times, an adult who paid a brief visit to their home would talk of "the sorrow" or "the grief" that surrounded them, and how unbearable it felt at times. And the last spark of empathy for others that was left in their hearts would feel for Yunie, who must have had to have gone through this awful experience for her entire life, knowing nothing else. But that was just it; Yunie hadn't known anything else besides what the grown-ups called sadness. She didn't really know what it was. Had nothing to compare it to. Most times, she would just feel empty. Like a beautifully crafted jug meant for use on special occasions such as this *Christmas*, but forgotten, left on a high shelf out of sight, never to be filled with anything other than a thick layer of melancholy dust.

She and her father continued to wade through the snow.

'Father?' Yunie piped up after a while.

'Yes, my love?' Lothar responded.

'What does it feel like? To be happy?'

Lothar stopped in his tracks now and looked up to the sky, once again apparently searching for the answer there.

'It's difficult to say,' he said. 'It's been so long since I truly felt it.'

'When was the last time?' Yunie asked.

Lothar looked at her now. His face suggested a torn confusion, as though he had only now realised that he had lost that thing called joy and had little or no idea where to look for it among his vast memories. He looked past her now and to the snow at her feet, his wide eyes darting left and right, the white frozen breath escaping his mouth in heavy puffs. Eventually he closed his mouth, his eyes stopped their quick movements back and forth and fixed on her steadily once more. When he spoke, his words came slowly, and almost detached from the meaning they were supposed to hold.

'As long as there is hope, there is still at least a little joy in a person. Joy at the very thought that all is not yet lost, and that we still have reason to move forwards.'

Yunie looked at her father and pondered this for a while in silence. Lothar's words held meaning, but Yunie knew that much of it was mysterious to her now. Perhaps would always be. But she knew about hope, although this too was a difficult concept for her, especially at such a young age. Hope was a word that clung to her, stuck to her memories like a boot is stuck to a swollen foot that's been trudging through the snow for too long.

'Do you still have some hope?' Yunie asked, eventually.

Lothar looked at his child with the same eyes that she had always known. Tired. Sad. Lost. He held his hand out to her.

'Come on,' he said. 'I'll make you a nice cup of tea.'

~

Back on the mountain, in the cabin that was now filled with a warm glow from the fireplace, Joy jumped but was not fully back with Yunie, in the present. Something strange was happening. The scene of Yunie and Lothar was fading but she saw them again somewhere else. Later, she thought, but not by much. Yunie looked almost the same. They were back in their old house in the village. But now Lothar was leading her out of it. She could hear their voices, but they were very distant. As distant as the ancient carol she had heard upon leaving the village behind.

But why, Father? Why are you going up the mountain?

He's there, Yunie.

Who's there?

The one who... the one who started it all.

Started what? How do you know he's there?

We don't have much time, Yunie. You're fading, and so am I. If I don't go now, it may be too late for both of us.

I don't want to go. I want to stay here.

Yunie! You must come.

What's the point? You can't fix anything.

The image of the father and daughter was fading again. But Joy could still hear their distant voices.

What's the point? I'll just stay here. I'm tired. I want to go to bed.

Now Joy could see Yunie a little more clearly. She was watching her through the eyes of Lothar. Lothar stood at the front door of the house, looking in at Yunie, who had come to the door but now sat on the floor, almost directly underneath the door frame. The image blurred again, but differently this time. Lothar blinked and the image became a little clearer.

Then he looked to the sky. It was daytime but the clouded sky was darkening. Snow was falling heavily. Somehow, through the thick cloud, he could see what looked like the brightest, shining star. He turned to Yunie again.

'Look, Yunie. Look! A Christmas star in the sky!'

Yunie looked interestedly up to the sky, and her little eyes widened in amazement. And for once she looked just how a child should look. Bright, inquisitive, almost joyful. But certainly *hopeful*. Her mouth opened slightly as she looked at the star.

Lothar looked back to it now too, and saw that it looked as though it was falling. Indeed, it hurtled towards the ground to the south and disappeared.

In the distance, he could almost swear he heard it crash.

He looked back to Yunie. Some colour had returned to her face, as though she herself had been one of those bleak, black and white drawings she'd been creating in previous days, and now she'd finally decided to colour herself in and become one with happiness once more. And at last he knew his daughter again.

'If that is not hope, I don't know what it is,' he said, and managed to smile as he spoke. 'Come, my daughter.'

Yunie took her father's hand, and the scene began to blur once more.

Joy regained some of her own thoughts.

Two strong memories competing for my attention. Yunie's and Lothar's.

She felt Lothar's coming through much more strongly now. She could see it forming. It was back to the day where Lothar had made breakfast and told Yunie about Christmas. Now she would see things from the mind of Lothar.

Relaxing, she let the memory take hold.

~

Lothar stoked the fire. The house was warm. Warmer than it had been for some time. He and Yunie had taken off their boots and set them by the fireplace to dry. Yunie now sat on the floor, as still as the great grey cloud above the village.

The kettle whistled, announcing that the water was ready. Lothar poured into two mugs he had prepared with herbs and berries. Instantly, the house was filled with a pleasant and sweet aroma.

'Come, Yunie, sit with me at the table. You must be careful with hot tea.'

Yunie got to her feet and took the chair beside her father.

'Let it cool a little,' Lothar said.

The child lowered her head and sniffed slowly at the mug.

'It smells wonderful,' she said.

Lothar smiled. 'I'm glad you think so.'

He stood up now and walked to the opposite side of the room where he opened an old storage box before rummaging around inside. He heard Yunie's intrigued voice ask him what he was doing, and he smiled.

'There's a part of Christmas that all children love,' he said. 'I want to present it to you now, for the first time.'

Finding what he was looking for, he closed the box and strolled back towards the table where his daughter regarded him and the smaller, wrapped up box with questioning eyes.

'What's this?' Yunie asked.

'It's a gift,' Lothar said, still smiling and now taking a seat again at the table. 'A Christmas gift. For you.'

Yunie looked at the thing. It was wrapped in brown paper and her father had tied a thin red bow around it in an elegant pattern on the top.

'It's...' Yunie began. 'It's very nice. Thank you.'

Then Lothar actually began to laugh. The sound of it seemed to alarm Yunie, who jumped and looked at her father as though he had just uttered some queer sound that was totally foreign.

'Oh, my sweet little girl!' Lothar said, still chuckling. 'The box is not your gift. Your gift is *inside*. You have to open it.'

'Open it?' Yunie said. 'How?'

Lothar gently picked his daughter's hands up from the table and placed them on the bow. He helped her to squeeze them around it and pull, allowing it to come free and fall soundlessly to the table.

'Now tear the paper,' Lothar said. 'It's okay, we shan't need it again. Tear it open!'

Yunie did as Lothar suggested, and soon she found a clear, closed box. Upon her father's further instruction, she opened the lid of it and reached inside. What she pulled out caused her to produce more of the confused looks on her face that had become so common on this day.

'What is it?' she asked.

'It's a toy,' Lothar said. 'At least, I think it is anyway.'

Yunie laid it on the table. It was a large metallic hand. At the wrist, it looked broken. Peculiar threads hung loosely out of the bottom of it. The hand itself was intricately crafted; if it weren't for the silver colour or the clear feel of steel, it might indeed have passed for a real hand.

'What do you do with it?' Yunie asked, vacantly.

'Well…' Lothar began, pulling a rather confused face of his own. 'I imagine you can come up with all sorts of things. Those types of toys became popular as I was growing up. I had a wind-up toy once, for a Christmas gift. It's funny, I can't seem to recall what happened to it.'

There was a cold silence in the room for a moment.

'Thank you, Father,' Yunie eventually broke it. She sounded sincere in her thanks. Perhaps she understood. That it wasn't about the gift itself but in the giving of it. In the celebration of having someone to love. To share things with. Even if it was merely an old metal hand which had been found near the foot of the great mountain.

'Your tea,' Lothar said. 'It should be cool enough to sip now.'

Yunie carefully lifted her mug to her lips and took a small sip of the tea. Noticing her father watching with keen interest, she nodded her head slightly and said, 'Mmm. It's good.'

Lothar took a sip of his own. The tea did indeed taste nice. Bitter yet sweet. He had no idea what herbs he had used, but they went well with the rest of the flavours inside the mug. Yunie was so impressed with it that she took a few further sips from the tea and stared almost blankly at the hand on the table.

'Are you hungry?' Lothar asked.

Yunie looked up from the hand. 'A little,' she said.

Lothar tried his best to smile once more, but the effort was becoming more arduous.

'Then we must have our Christmas dinner.'

***

It was a meagre meal. Lothar showed Yunie how to bake bread, but today being Christmas, he put some of the berries he'd used in the tea into the mix. The result was a sweet bread which he served with some of the same fish they'd had for breakfast. The eggs had run out. During their meal he told Yunie about the Christmas crackers her grandmother used to make. How she'd fill them with colour and how the family used to look forward to reading out the messages inside.

Yunie listened with apparent interest but made no comment. She was looking to the window now. The sun had set and the only light was that from the fireplace, where the logs had almost burned out.

'Oh no,' Yunie said.

'What is it, my love?'

'It's snowing again.'

Lothar looked out the window and his heart also sank.

Bright spirits, Lothar. The child. Christmas day.

'It's alright,' he said, turning to Yunie. 'If I must carry you over the snow then I will.'

She showed no sign of having been encouraged by these words. She looked downheartedly out the window, the dying light from the fire highlighting the dismayed and increasingly empty look on her face. And Lothar's heart sank all the more to see it; to see his own daughter at such a young and tender age be so near to broken.

But was she really *broken* if she had never been one and whole in the first instance?

He felt helpless. Yunie didn't even know what she was missing out on, but the fact that life seemed to pass by her without so much as stopping for a moment to bestow the smallest piece of luck or good tidings upon her was a miserable affair.

She's almost gone. She's almost become what everyone else has. And she never even had one good Christmas.

'I'm tired,' Yunie said. 'I'm going to bed.'

***

He went with her. She said nothing of it. Didn't it seem odd?

She slumped into bed, wearing the same clothes she'd had on all day. She pulled the blankets up to her waist. Lothar pulled up a chair and tucked the blankets warmly up to Yunie's shoulders.

'Stay warm, my love.'

'Why do you call me that? Love? What's a love?'

Not for the first time that day, Lothar's spirit broke a little more.

'Love is the greatest thing that a person can offer to another.'

She stared at the ceiling, eyes wide open. They no longer looked tired.

'My mother – your grandmother – she always used to sing me to sleep on Christmas night with a carol.'

Yunie's eyes remained the same. Searching for some piece of the joy from her father's past that would enlighten her about it all. They darted sideways now and looked at Lothar.

'A carol? What carol would she sing?'

She remained inquisitive. Surely, this was a good thing? To be questioning was a form of hope, was it not? Hope of finding an answer to something. Hope of finding that little piece of joy.

'Many. But I had a favourite.'

'Sing me it. Please. Sing me your favourite carol.'

The cheek of Lothar's face which was turned away from his daughter became damp. Was this it? Was this the last spark of hope or joy left in his child? Was this the very last ounce of anything cheerful in her?

'Of course, my love. It would be my honour.'

He remembered the tune but he couldn't recall many of the words. He knew it started "silent night" but didn't know where it went afterwards. So he made up the words. He sang of love and cheer and endless amounts of hope. And when he was finished, Yunie was asleep.

Lothar didn't move. He looked at his daughter's chest silently moving up and down and wondered if she was dreaming, if she had ever dreamed at all in her short life. He didn't want to end it – the last good memory he had of his daughter. Singing her to sleep upon Christmas night with his favourite carol from years gone by.

So he stayed. He stayed by Yunie's bedside and watched her lightly breathing in and out. He gently wept for the oncoming death of the last good thing in this world. He felt bitter dejection begin to overwhelm him.

Eventually, he fell asleep in the chair. When they both awoke the next morning, Lothar barely knew his daughter.

5
Carol of the Bells

While Joy was somewhere at the bottom of the great mountain, searching for the very thing that was relentlessly seeping away from her, Lothar was near the end of his own journey to the top.

He had left Yunie in the cabin, now several feet below him. She'd followed him there, but this was no place for a child. No place at all. He had felt the last piece of what he could call either joy or hope begin to slip away, and it had stirred him to do something about it. It had been the old man, Eric, who had told him where he should look if he so felt the urge.

The top of the mountain, Lothar. I went there myself only yesterday. But know this, friend; you will not like what you find there.

He held a torch in his hand as he drove himself up the mountain. He could not think of Yunie, for when he did, he would find himself wanting to go back to her. He longed to climb into the bed in the cabin with her and sleep. Yes, just sleep. And would they ever wake? Mayhap they would. But perhaps not. And would he mind either way? Would Yunie?

He'd shake his head when his mind went there, attempting to physically shake the thought away.

Onwards. Ever onwards. To whatever was at the top of this blasted mountain.

To whatever end.

***

Later that night, Joy held Yunie in her arms and wept.

The child didn't move. She said nothing. She allowed this strange woman to hold her and openly weep for whatever reason. And what reason *was* it? Joy didn't quite know. A mixture of things; she wept because she had seen this young child first as a baby and then as an older child, and in all of that time she'd barely seen an ounce of happiness. She wept because although Yunie hardly knew it, she'd lost so much at such a young age – her mother, her grandparents, her aunt and uncle. Her father, perhaps. She wept because although Yunie was much younger, she somehow reminded her of her own lost sister, whom she'd never see or speak to again.

Your fault! Your fault!

She wept because she felt powerless. Utterly powerless. She knew the end was here, whatever happened. The summit of the mountain was close. She would soon reach it and find whatever it was that had caused all of this. She'd find out whether or not she was able to stop it.

But stopping it won't bring any of the dead ones back. It won't give Yunie the childhood she never had. It won't allow you to see Hope ever again. What's the point? Stay awhile longer, child from the failing stars. Stay and spend the last moments of your life weeping for a child lost in a universe void of the faintest spark of light.

She realised she was squeezing Yunie tightly, and loosened her grip a little in fear that she may have hurt the child.

'Yunie?' she whispered. Her voice was shaking. 'Yunie, can you talk to me?'

The child said nothing.

Joy held on to her, staring at the wall behind. 'Yunie, I know this all must seem so strange to you. If I had the words or the courage to explain, I would.'

The child said nothing.

'I'm going to have to leave you here. Just for a while. I'll make sure the fire is fresh. You should stay in the bed and keep warm. I'll come back for you. I promise.'

The child said nothing.

Joy let go of her now. Yunie looked blankly at the floor.

She's nearly gone! Old Hunter will be back here very soon. And oh! How he shall feast!

'Your father…' Joy began, looking at Yunie and bravely willing her tears to cease. 'Your father loves you very much. I don't know where he is now but wherever he is, whatever he's doing, it's for you, Yunie. And he'll come back for you. I know it. And you'll be happy to see him. Yes, you'll be *happy*.'

The child said nothing.

Joy set about making sure the fire was blazing warmly before gently setting Yunie down on her back in the soft, warm bed. She kissed her on the forehead and was glad to see that her eyes were slowly closing.

'I'm going now,' Joy said. 'I'm going to see your father.'

And then her eye caught something inside the bed, wrapped in the blanket as though it had done this itself and wanted to keep warm. Lothar's old bobin. Given to him as a baby. It was Yunie's now, and she'd somehow thought it a good idea to bring the soft toy along with her. Joy didn't know if her heart was warmed or broken by this. She picked it up and tucked it in beside Yunie.

'There,' she said. 'Hold on to your bobin. You can look after each other until I'm back. Keep it close. It will make you feel something like happy.'

The child said nothing.

Joy turned towards the door and set her hand on the handle. She was about to pull the door open when, from behind her, the child spoke.

'Go. Hope needs you.'

Before she could allow grief to overcome her, Joy opened the door, stepped out into the cold, and let her frozen tears mix with the softly cascading snowdrops.

***

Outside the cabin, the moons and the stars shone brilliantly upon the mountain. A pale light began to emerge in the sky. Dawn was near.

Her attention was suddenly grasped by a small, sweet chirping. She didn't see the bird coming, but felt Fortune as she landed in her usual spot on Joy's shoulder.

'Hello, my friend. When did you leave me?'

The wolf. Fortune must have fled once more at the sight of Woe.

'It's gone now,' Joy said. 'And it won't come back. Come on. Let's get up this mountain.'

In front of her, a wooden rope bridge stretched out across a large chasm. In past times, people must have come up the mountain for various reasons. She wondered how old the bridge was, but felt little fear at the thought of it breaking, sending her to the black oblivion below.

It creaked when she stepped on it, but she strode forwards with confidence and cleared the bridge easily in a matter of moments. On the other side, she stared upwards. The growing light ominously illuminated the mountain, and she could see now that there wasn't much further to climb. The path here was easier too; a set of old stairs had been built into the slope and just before the summit, Joy could see a cave of some sort. She felt her Sense pulling at her, crying that she'd found it. She'd finally found it. Within that cave were all the answers she'd been searching for all her life.

Her Sense also told her that Lothar had arrived there some time before, and had not liked what he'd found.

'And just like that, his memories come to me again,' Joy said to Fortune as she felt them near. But this time she didn't let them fully take her. She kept walking forwards, slowly and with half-closed eyes. She was nearly there. What use would more memory really be now? She stepped onto the first icy stair and saw pictures flash by in her head as she went.

A young boy pulling a sledge through the snow. There are many other children riding down a great slope behind him, laughing heartily and full of the deepest, purest joy. But this boy is a little different. This boy wears a deep, hurt frown on his face.

Step.

Before Joy could wonder about it the image disappears. In its place she sees a young man. But this doesn't look like Lothar. He's too tall. He walks differently. This is someone else entirely. He's in an extravagant place; a castle or a palace of some sort. A great hall lined with long banners at each wall. There are many people here. Again, they all seem happy. Except this man. Unlike the others he sits at a table alone while everyone else talks animatedly among themselves and appear to be congratulating each other. The man here and the boy before are the same person? Who is he? Why is Joy suddenly seeing this?

Step.

The memories push forwards. The man is older now. He sits at a table, on which is set a machine of some sort. He's using a tool to carefully adjust something. And for the first time, Joy hears a sound coming from this memory. A woman's voice somewhere unseen. It utters one word which bounces off the walls of the mountain as she climbs.

'Ludwig?'

He glances up from his work for a mere second before going back to it. In that brief second Joy could see the woman who called. She's beautiful, but her face tells the same old story of dejection and misery that Joy has known all her years. As this man, this Ludwig, goes back to his machine, the memory begins to fade again.

Step.

Now Ludwig sits with a different machine all together. It looks like a large glass ball set on top of a small pillar made from stone. Inside is darkness, but the tiniest glimmer of light is floating around, lonely. Ludwig stares inside it with a blank expression. The tiny dot of light appears to swim in the darkness and bounce off the inside of the glass before returning once again to the middle. Ludwig turns and examines something on the wall. A humanoid figure made from metal.

Step.

She can't see the man now, but she's looking at a battlefield. It takes place on a flat piece of land with mountains in the distance. Several of the metal people race forwards and aim rifles at humans. The humans fight back but it's not going well. Several men and women fire and land their shots accurately on the torsos and heads of the metal ones. The bullets mostly bounce off and do no harm. But the biggest difference Joy can see is in the faces of the combatants. The humans have looks of sorrow, misery, depression. The metal people hold no emotion. And the longer this fight goes on, Joy understands, the more the humans will become just like the robots.

Step.

Ludwig, once again at his glass ball. This time the darkness is almost gone and the tiny flickers of light have grown and formed a ball of their own inside. Joy, through Ludwig, stares into it. They see things. People. Faces. All of them bright, all of them happy, but trapped inside this contraption. They see families, children, joy. Now nothing more than myths from long ago. Ludwig steps away from it. He's much older now. Grey hair and deep lines set into a face which somehow represents a grim sadness much more profound than Joy has ever known.

Step.

She reached the top of the staircase. A short walk ahead of her, the mouth of the cave that held all the answers awaited.

The end of it.

***

By the time Joy had set her first foot inside the cave, the sun had begun to appear from behind her, illuminating the cave in a warm glow. She walked forwards cautiously, not knowing what in the world to expect inside. Even Fortune seemed nervous; she uttered a stifled tweet which echoed and bounced off the stone walls around them.

'Ssshhh,' Joy said, quietly. 'Hush, Fortune. We don't know who, or what may be in here.'

Except, hopefully, Lothar.

The further inside the cave she went, the darker it became. Her own soft footsteps sounded loudly throughout the place, and became louder still as the stone around them contained the noise and shut off anything from the outside.

'Your eyes will no doubt be better than mine,' Joy said to the bobin. 'I wish you could speak. Then you'd be able to tell me what's ahead.'

They kept going. Fortune's head darted this way and that, possibly looking at whatever was now surrounding them, possibly panicking that she could see nothing through the immense darkness. But something told Joy to keep going – just a little further and the darkness wouldn't be a problem anymore.

Her Sense was right. A few steps further and the tunnel they'd found themselves in opened up ahead into a large space which looked to be lit with a white light. It was still, not flickering. This was no fire. Approaching slowly, Joy began to hear voices. She couldn't make out what they were saying, but she could tell that there were at least two people up ahead. They were men, and they were talking with very little emotion in their voices.

This is it… Time to find out what I came here for. Oh, sister, I hope it wasn't in vain.

One more step forward brought into view the thing which had made so much light. It was the glass ball she'd seen in those peculiar flashes of memory. Ludwig's memories. In here it was again set upon a sort of stone dais. But the ball was now *filled* with light. It was so packed that Joy couldn't see any of it move at all, as it had done before. The light was so strong that she had to scrunch up her eyes and shield them with a hand until they became used to the intense radiance.

When her eyes stopped hurting, she saw a man sitting with his back to the far wall of the opening in the cave.

'Lothar!'

She ran towards him. He looked tired and hurt. His eyes had been fixed on the orb of light in front of him, but now regarded Joy curiously. When she reached him, she crouched down beside him and instinctively grasped his hand in hers.

'Do I know you?' he asked.

Joy couldn't help but smile a sad, tearful smile. 'No. But I know you.'

Lothar looked ever more confused. He said nothing.

'It would take a long time to explain,' Joy said. 'And I'm afraid time is not something we have very much of. My name is Joy.'

'*Joy!?*' another voice spat. It was cold, grim. Full of malice. Joy spun round and found a tall, old man with an irascible aura protruding from him.

'Oh, that is ironic,' the old man said. 'Almost poetic.'

'Ludwig,' Joy said. 'Your name is Ludwig.'

He looked at her with ardent interest now. 'How would you know a thing like that?'

Joy stood up and faced him. 'As I was saying to Lothar, it would take too long to explain.'

Ludwig stepped forward. The light from the orb showed him in more detail. He had lost much of his hair, but now had a thick, grey beard. He wore a large fur coat which looked to Joy as though it had seen better days. His face remained hard and unflinching, like a great lighthouse standing defiantly against the waves of a stormy sea.

'You're not from here, are you?' Ludwig said, coldly.

'No.' Joy returned. 'You could say my home is...'

'Beyond the stars?' Ludwig finished for her. Joy's heart leapt and Ludwig seemed to notice and to take some satisfaction from it. 'Oh, yes. I'm well aware that there are other worlds out there. Never did think I'd *meet* someone from one of them, mind you.'

'How?' Joy said. 'How can you know that? This planet doesn't have the technology...'

'No,' Ludwig agreed. 'But it might have done some day. Too bad, really. The thought of life from other worlds has been nothing but a child's dream here.'

Joy was taken aback by this. She hadn't expected to discuss something of this nature. She came here expecting to find out what had happened to happiness, not to be discussing life on other planets with a man who, by all likelihood, should know nothing of such matters. She almost had no idea what to say next. Except, she had one burning question:

'What is this ball?'

Ludwig scoffed and turned to look at it. 'It's joy. And by the looks of it, it's just about all the joy in the universe.'

'You mean…' Joy started. '*This* is what's been happening to it? People have been losing their sense of joy and happiness, and it's somehow ended up in this glass ball of yours?'

Ludwig smirked now. 'This *glass ball* as you put it, made it all happen.'

'And who made the ball?'

Ludwig frowned now. 'Come now, child. You're an intelligent thing. I've seen your people, you know. Watched them from my best telescope. I would know nothing of them, of course, if it hadn't been for all of your marvellous flying machines. Dwindled in numbers ever since my ball started collecting joy, though.'

Joy might perhaps have questioned Ludwig on this; on how he could possibly have known anything about her planet, known about the spacecrafts and presumably that Joy herself had come here piloting one of them. She might have let curiosity ask the questions it desperately wanted to, but something about hearing this vile old man even mention her home, mention how it had once been full of joy, talk of the lack of spacecrafts surrounding it with almost a gloating tone, made anger well up inside her.

'How dare you,' Joy said. 'How dare you mention my home. You've taken everything from it. *Everything!*'

She turned and looked at Lothar, who still sat slumped with his back against the stone wall of the cave. Was he gone now? Did he have nothing left?

'And here,' Joy said, facing Ludwig once again. 'You've done the same to everyone on this planet too. Your own people, I have to assume. You built this strange contraption of yours with the purpose of sucking away everyone's happiness. *Why?* Why would anyone want to do that?'

Ludwig looked away from Joy. His eyes now fixed upon the ball, watching the light within. Joy did the same, and now she could see flashes of memories within. She saw many people; some looked familiar to her in shape and appearance, but others came from alien worlds far away from here, ones that even the observation department of Gylfandell knew nothing of. All of these memories were bright, wholesome and full of the purest form of joy.

Trapped forever inside a glass ball of misery.

She looked at Ludwig again. 'You're not going to tell me, are you? You don't even have the decency to tell me why you've done this?'

'Why do you want to know?' a grim voice sounded from the entrance to the tunnel that Joy had earlier come through. She didn't need to look, or to notice Fortune once again hurrying away from her shoulder to find a safer spot somewhere in the darkness to know what had arrived.

'Woe,' Joy said with spite in her voice. 'What do you want?'

The great wolf was almost too big to fit inside the tunnel. His great black body almost looked stuck in place as he stood, eyes fixed gravely on Joy.

'I am *Hunter*,' the wolf argued. 'And I have tracked down my next meal. If you would be so kind to step aside, I would feast upon the father before the daughter.'

'And I would die fighting you before I allowed you to go near this man!' Joy said. She stood tall, even took a step towards the wolf. But she had no plan. What in the wide universe she thought she would be able to do against a massive creature like this wolf, she had no idea. But she was nonetheless resolute; she faced the wolf, trembling, terrified, but unmoving.

Woe shook the walls of the enclosure with howling, wicked laughter.

'It would be a pity,' the wolf said. 'If I had to kill you before you'd reached your peak depression. But I will if I must. And anyway, there's a rather much younger prize that you left down in the cabin across the rope bridge. Her time is nearly up. I daresay she will make a splendid last meal before I move on to another world.'

Fury filled Joy like a wild storm that uproots the widest and strongest of tress from the cold, hard ground.

'You will not touch her! By whatever strength is left in me, I will stop you, *Woe!*'

The wolf snarled, baring jagged teeth as sharp as the finest of blades on this planet or the next. Joy's heart was beating so rapidly, with each beat coming so quickly after the last that it was almost as though it wasn't beating at all; as though it had shocked itself into stopping completely, knowing the end had surely come.

Woe advanced. Joy closed her eyes. Waiting. The whole area was filled with a tension and an apprehension so heavy that Joy became lost in it, and forgot for a moment where she was at all.

And then the space was filled with something else entirely. It stopped Woe in its tracks. The wolf's ears pricked upwards and its head turned towards the peculiar sound that now filled the air.

Birdsong. Sweet, pure, innocent and melodic birdsong. Joy opened her eyes again and saw that Fortune had perched herself on a piece of rock that had jutted out from the wall of the cave, and was now standing upright on her skinny little legs, head proudly raised, eyes closed and beak open. But this wasn't her usual sound; gone were the urgent and sometimes fearful or sad tweets. This was most certainly *singing*. It was tuneful, and Joy instantly recognised the song.

So too, did Lothar, whose head raised in remembrance. For how couldn't he? He had sung it himself not so very long ago, on Christmas night. Yunie had fallen asleep to it. Of course, there were no words to this version, but the first two words that Joy remembered Lothar sing resonated and happily sang in her own mind:

Silent night…

It was beautiful. The bobin sang the tune with perfect intonation, and delightfully trilled the long notes, which rang out across the whole cave and, Joy was sure of it, carried off down the mountainside, perhaps even to Lothar's village. Maybe even some way, somehow, it floated away from this planet altogether and carried light years across the universe. In that splendid moment, Joy could envision this lovely music carrying all the way to her sister's ears in Gylfandell. The power of this little bird's song was so immense that Joy almost allowed herself to believe that it had cured the universe of its sadness, and brought a fresh light to the hearts of all of those who had spent countless years of their lives in bleak suffering.

She was snapped back to reality with the next words of the wolf.

'What is this?' it spat, looking up at the bird with a scowl.

And then Joy realised. It came to her like a final jolt to her senses. She suddenly knew what Fortune was doing.

'Beautiful, isn't it?' Joy said to Woe. 'Fills your spirit with all kinds of things. Memory, tranquillity… but joy most of all, I would say.'

Woe spun back and faced Joy again. In its eyes, Joy could see a flicker of panic. She was right.

'*What?*' the wolf growled. 'What did you say?'

Joy calmly advanced on the wolf now. The wolf began to back off.

'I said that the bobin's singing makes me *happy,*' Joy said. 'You know, joyful. Cheerful. Thankful for life and everything in it.'

'Silence!' Woe barked. 'Stay away from me and I'll make your death swift!'

'Death?' Joy asked, and managed a small laugh. 'There will be no death here, Woe. Not today.'

'Silence!!' Woe repeated, voice now shaking. 'Get back!'

'You see,' Joy continued, coolly. 'I named you *Woe* because I felt pity for you. Pity because where there is woe, there is no joy. But that works both ways. Woe cannot exist in a world where one remembers the things that bring joy. Like my sister, Hope.'

'Be quiet!!' Woe cried. 'I demand it!!'

'Yes,' Joy remarked. 'Sometimes it's difficult. Especially when everything seems so grim. But I think of my sister and she brings me hope. And courage. And most of all, happiness.'

The wolf cried out now, seemingly in pain. Woe's head now lolled lazily to one side, and to Joy's astonishment, she saw that it now began to fade.

'Curse you!!' Woe cried. 'Curse you, Joy!!'

And by the time Fortune had finished her wonderful song, Woe had disappeared into the darkness.

***

Now then, Joy thought, sleepily. *Now to get to the bottom of all of this.*

She breathed out slowly and turned to find the old man Ludwig standing by his glass ball, standing with that same grim expression, standing and watching. Further behind him, at the other side of the glowing ball, Lothar got to his feet. The song of Fortune had awoken him, but perhaps only temporarily.

'Will you tell me then?' Joy asked, looking Ludwig in his cold eyes. 'Will you tell me why you've done this? Why you've seized joy from the universe?'

Ludwig made no sound. He stood looking at Joy, his face now expressionless but worn.

'Very well,' Joy said. 'Give me a minute. I'll find out for myself.'

Ludwig's face changed now. Joy's words had clearly startled and confused him. He may have known something of Joy's home world, but it seemed he knew nothing of the Sense. But oh, what memories were trying desperately to come through to Joy now! Many, many of them, fighting for her attention, crying out to be seen and to be heard. And Joy would love nothing more than to switch off for an hour or two and really experience these memories, find out exactly what had happened on this planet and how it had spread to so many others.

But she couldn't. Time was quickly running out. Fortune's song had lit enough of a spark in both her and Lothar to dispose of the great wolf, but joy was still vanishing, regardless. She could feel it within herself now, the last logs of a dying fire sending out its final bleak smoke, set to vanish somewhere among the departing and lonesome stars. Ghosts were all she had time for now. Vapid ghosts of distant memories, bells tolling for their final time, carried by the wind to another world where they would be heard only by those who were really listening out for them, and who would only weep to hear their tales of empty loss.

'What do you mean?' Ludwig asked. But he was too late. Joy had already closed her eyes and had gone in search of those hazy memories which she hoped would tell all.

~

A man. No, not a man, a *thing*. A being appeared in front of Joy. The being was running. Fast. Faster than Joy had seen man, woman, child or beast run; quicker than a bobin, swifter than a cat. In its face (*Face? Was it really a face?*) it held a look of tired desperation. How long had it been running, and why so furiously? How its legs must have ached and its lungs must have burned! Turning its head, it spotted Joy and immediately halted. Was this the first time it had stopped running in all its long years of life? Its eyes (*Eyes? Were they really eyes?*) widely expanded and Joy knew that the being was regretful in having been spotted. It did what it had to do; it turned, bowed its head (*Head?*) low and raced back the way it came. It made no sound as it did so but Joy could see that the sprint back came at a great effort. *Don't make me do it! Don't make me!* It shrank as it went but the lines on its – *face?* – lessened and its – *eyes?* – became younger. And then Joy understood; each step backwards was a step recalled through a weary and difficult life. Each step was a painful reminder – no, not a *reminder...* a reliving – a reliving of a burning, bitter existence. She was no longer sure she wanted to know, but she watched the being as it transformed and its head, its face, its eyes became the features of an unmistakably young version of Ludwig, sitting at a desk and writing with a quill. In those newly reformed old eyes, Joy saw that much of the same anguish and dejection of the adult version was still prominent. But there was an undeniable innocence, a faint glimmer of something close to hope, of which Joy knew the importance, and oh! If only someone could reach out to this boy now and rescue it, hold it close and never let it go, protect it as though it was the final flame upon the last candle of joy out in a wild snowstorm. But she knew. Yes, she knew. The boy's light would go out, and she could only watch how it would happen, and hopelessly hope that she could learn something from it.

***

Joy could hear nothing, but just as an old photograph may tell a story of many words, even to those who were never around in the time of its taking, the images she saw painted a clear, painful picture.

Ludwig was lonely. He sat in the classroom of what looked to Joy an old school. There were no other children here, just Ludwig. His quill worked furiously at some mathematics, or language, or whatever it was that children studied so profusely in this place. The image was cloudy but it begged Joy to fully consume it, and she knew that if she let it, she would lose herself in the memory and she would experience it as clearly as she had those with Lothar and Yunie.

No! Mustn't let it. Can't leave Lothar in the cave.

Suddenly an old man appeared. He looked strikingly similar to the Ludwig Joy knew in the present. The young Ludwig was comforted by this man's presence. A fatherly sort of figure? No... the word *father* seemed a painful word for Ludwig. What then? Mentor. Ah, yes. This word fit perfectly.

Ludwig's mentor observed the work he had written onto his parchment and commended him on such a remarkable job. Science. This was some form of science. Joy couldn't understand exactly what kind, but she might have guessed this; the young boy would grow up to become an inventor of some sort, wouldn't he?

The scene faded and now Joy saw Ludwig arrive at a small house. He took his coat off and hung it on a hook to the side of the front door and began to quietly walk further inside when he was stopped by that *father* who inspired so much fear and anxiety within the boy. He was angry. Something about wasting his time writing stories when he should have been home clearing a path through the snow. Didn't the boy know that it had been snowing all the long day?

Silent voices raised, and Ludwig trembled. He knew what was coming next and he hoped that it would be mercifully brief. Today it was a hard smack across the cheek and a kick to the already bruised ribcage. He ran to his bedroom after this to weep in silence, and to try to imagine his hunger away. There would be no dinner for Ludwig tonight. Instead, when he had finished crying, he turned to his many books for comfort and read deep into the night by the light of a small candle.

The being, the headless, faceless, eyeless thing, picked up the pace.

Ludwig was now a little older, but still a child. Many mournful bodies were gathered around a grave, dressed in black. They looked grimly upon not one, but two coffins as they were lowered into the cold ground. Ludwig was not looking. He'd turned his back and kept his eyes fixed upon a single purple flower he held in his hand. The emotion he felt was too mixed and confusing for him.

His parents. Both of them. Killed in a terrible accident with a horse and carriage. Yes, his father had been a brute, but his *mother*...

He lived with his uncle now, who presently stood by his side and placed a kind hand on his shoulder. He said something to his nephew that Joy couldn't hear, but was again nonetheless clear to her.

Do not fret, lad. Mourn while you must. I'll be here at your side.

And as lovely as these words truly were, Joy could not help but feel somewhere significant in her heart they would become another form of grief for the young boy. And as though in confirmation of the point, she saw Ludwig's uncle begin to cough, and knew that this dry, painful gasp was the beginning of more heartache.

The being sped forwards. Ever forwards.

Ludwig was a young man now, and the grim face that Joy easily recognised was already etched into his face, set in a deep stone that would bear the rough years to come. He was alone inside a dark room, using a tool to fix a piece of iron onto a large board which looked electrical to Joy, though she knew that it couldn't possibly be... could it?

The room was a busy mess of things, most of which looked expensive and elaborate. There were several desks with pieces of parchment strewn all over them, strange objects dotted around, microscopes and other scientific equipment to be seen everywhere. Beside a large circular window, a telescope stood pointing upwards to the stars. Beside this was a table which held a battered old book, an ink pot and a quill. It seemed Ludwig had been very busy in these days.

His head turned sharply towards the door, and Joy understood that there had been a knock. When he called out for the person to enter, the door swung open and a woman around the same age as Ludwig arrived. Ludwig had quickly returned to his work, but Joy wondered whether if, had he been looking at the woman, he might have seen the sorrowful look on her face.

Small talk. A dance around the subject the woman was reluctant to arrive at. And then:

Your uncle is dead. Died in the night... Don't you want to come and see him?

Ludwig did. Of course he did. It was just that he had important work to do here. He was nearly at a breakthrough. Just a few more long nights of tireless work and...

He'd barely noticed that the woman was gone. The room had grown ever darker. He paused in his work only to light more candles. His work continued.

The running man (or *not* man), that being with the face (*no* face?) and eyes (*what eyes??*) stopped for a moment and turned his head – his thing that *might* have been his "head".

Yes. He stopped. First time in... how long? Oh, many a year. He stopped because now he knew. Now, having lived this life once before and known all the pain and suffering within it, he knew that this was the moment. The moment that everything might have changed for the better.

Joy saw that time had frozen, and not just here in this dreamlike world where she visited the memories of others. In this strange half-observation half-remaining in the real world, she could distantly see Lothar, and Fortune, and Ludwig as an old man. They stood as still as planks, watching Joy with frozen interest. In Ludwig's memory, the door had just shut as the woman had left, and young Ludwig stood stiffly, inspecting some metal object in his hand.

Joy could feel the being's anguish. And just like the memories, she heard no sound but she knew very well what this being was saying.

Now, you fool!! Now!! If you just go after her, tell her you're sorry, tell her you love her, she'll stay with you! You won't have to be lonely, you won't have to be sad. Go now! Go!!

And Joy knew that this voice had no hope of actually getting through to the Ludwig of the past. It was just an unleashing of thoughts and feelings that had long been bottled up and were now exploding into nothingness. The being was curled up into a ball now and wailing in agony. She wondered if it might just stay there. It had nothing else to live for anyway, did it? And it could well just stop time in the universe and trap it inside this eternal misery forever. Except for her; she was somehow exempt from being caught in this time net. She was free to roam around. And that's all she'd be able to do. Wander this sad, lonesome planet devoid of all happiness, watching the frozen final moments of all who had lingered, never being able to move on herself.

She needn't have worried about it. The being came to his senses and walked a few steps first before turning once more to a full, grief-stricken sprint. As the faceless one moved achingly onwards, Joy now only saw brief glimpses into Ludwig's past. The being moved so rapidly past this time that Joy thought it must really have not wanted to relive this part. It all looked very monotonous now; Ludwig in his study, looking through his telescope or scribbling things down or studying books. She saw no hint of any family or friends, no sign of happiness in this lonely man's life. And then the being slowed a little, and Joy could tell that it had arrived at a memory so painful, so crushingly unhappy that it clung to the being and *begged* to be remembered.

Remember me! Yes, remember me! Never forget! For I will be with you for all time. And beyond.

Not much further into Ludwig's future, Joy saw him once again at work in his study, and once again a knock came at the door. Ludwig seemed confused at this. He opened the door slowly and found two people, a man and a woman of authority, something like soldiers or police officers, Joy thought. And with them was a child. A young girl no older than five or six. She looked very sad.

The female officer spoke first. Joy understood that she was confirming Ludwig's identity. Ludwig nodded and affirmed that he was who they suspected. The male officer asked if they might come inside. Ludwig agreed, still with much confusion upon his face. And then he saw it. The face of this child. It was remarkable. It was like looking into a mirror from the past. Ludwig's hair had not been so long, nor his eyes so exceptionally bright, and never, ever had he set about a smile on his face in times of grief or anxiety as this child bravely did, but her face was undoubtedly his own.

The female officer took the child to an area of Ludwig's study where she might not hear the conversation between the two men, who now sat at chairs in front of the large window where a clear night sky showed off the twinkling stars of distant galaxies, one of which, Joy knew, was her own.

Ludwig guessed much of what had happened, but the officer explained the situation to him regardless. The girl was Ludwig's daughter, the only child of a relationship which had faltered some years prior. Her only family had been a mother and a father. She had nobody else.

What had happened to her mother? Joy could almost hear the soundless words coming from the male officer's mouth as he whispered them:

Well, it's a strange thing indeed. Those who knew her said that she had become distant. Quiet. As though a great sadness had come alive and wrapped itself around her. She stopped speaking in time, and she became quite sick with it. Eventually she just closed her eyes and never woke up again.

Ludwig looked over to the child. *His* child. She was happily in conversation with the female officer. She must have witnessed it. The deterioration of her mother, happiness taken from her bit by bit until nothing was left but an empty vessel of what was once her mother. How terrible. And yet she smiled. She smiled because... because of what? What in this wide world did she have reason to smile for?

The being observed this scene silently now. He stood motionless, as though time had frozen once again, and yet the past moved on. Memory flowed onwards.

Ludwig didn't know how to be a father. He'd had no interest in such things. And now this young girl was suddenly with him. He immersed himself in his work, ignoring the child. She didn't seem to mind; she wandered her father's study and inquisitively watched him work. Her mother was never the subject of the few and rare conversations that they had. But still, she made no fuss.

Joy watched with the being as day by day came and went. Ludwig worked and his daughter watched. Until one day, she finally mentioned her mother. Being an innocent child, she wondered if her father really ever knew her mother. Ludwig confirmed that he did, and then continued scribbling away on a piece of parchment. And then Joy once again could almost hear words of a conversation buried deep in this memory. The child asked:

What's under there?

She had indicated a large piece of cloth on top of a table, which looked to be covering something circular.

It's just something I'm working on. That's all.
Can I see?

With a sigh, Ludwig removed the cloth, and Joy's heart leapt. It was the ball. The glass ball she could see both here in Ludwig's memory, empty and dark, and in Joy's present, filled and glowing brightly.

What's it for?
You're too young to understand.

But it just so happened that a few days later, the child once again talked of her mother, and of how sad she had become in her final days. She had been sad, the child said, because she was lonely. And even though she had the happiest, loveliest and cleverest little girl in the whole world, sometimes nothing could stop the great monster known as sadness. It had been like a poison. A poison which had entered into their lives and had changed it so devastatingly.

As she told her father this, Ludwig looked into the face of his daughter and once again saw himself there. Only, she was much more beautiful than he. Her great, sad eyes twinkled like the stars that Ludwig had studied for so long. And that was when he knew. Yes, of course he loved the child. *His* child. Loved her deeply. And he couldn't let her be so sad.

My dear daughter. Let me show you what that ball of mine might do.

He had her stand next to it and close her eyes. He told her to think of something happy. A time she could remember about with her mother. The child thought of last Christmas. Baking gingerbread with her mother. Ludwig turned the ball slightly and watched, heart racing. A single bright light seemed to escape from the child's chest and enter the ball. She opened her eyes and saw it.

Wow! It's so pretty! What is it?

It's your memory. It's here, in the ball. Touch it.

She placed a fingertip lightly to the glass and gasped.

I can see it! I can see it, Father!

And Ludwig was as ecstatic as his daughter was.

You can come here and see your mother any time. And should you think of more memories you'd like to keep forever, just return to the ball and think them. Same as you did just now.

And the child did. Often. The being began a slow, lethargic walk onwards now, headless head drawn sadly downwards, eyeless eyes downcast miserably. The child began filling the ball with memory after memory, and Ludwig watched on with happiness; happiness that his daughter had a way to remember her mother, and happiness that his machine worked. A memory machine! How this will change the world! The universe!

But over the coming days and weeks, the child became distant. With each memory she placed inside the ball, she seemed to become sadder. And Ludwig at first didn't realise what would become, in the years of replaying these memories in his head, exceptionally obvious: the child wasn't simply *storing* her memories. She was losing them.

The ball had at this point been filled with a glowing, yellow light. When Ludwig asked his daughter about her mother, a confused look came upon her face.

My dear... Don't you remember? Gingerbread at Christmas?

The child said nothing.

The being was glowing with grief. But he marched on, faceless face veiled by a dark cloud of misery.

He stopped at the worst memory.

Even Joy could not see this properly. This memory was scarred. As though someone, Ludwig or the being had tried to scratch it out of existence. But it played on like a miserable story that would be retold eternally.

Night. Ludwig sat in his chair by a fire. A door creaked open. His daughter. She had lost her smile now. She stepped towards the glowing ball.

No, my love. We talked about this. You mustn't use it anymore. Better we get rid of the thing.

The child seemed to agree. Reaching out, she pushed the ball firmly. It rolled from the table...

No!!

... and dropped to the hard floor beneath, shattering. The light from within burst out and raced towards the child, disappearing inside her chest as she collapsed to the floor.

Ludwig ran to her. Her wide eyes darted to and fro, madly.

What have you done, my daughter!?

And she was smiling.

I got them back! My memories! I can see her again. Gingerbread at Christmas...

She closed her eyes. They never opened again.

Joy sped along with the being, leaving Ludwig cradling his little girl in his study. The being moved faster again and now took them to a dark room, several years in the future. Ludwig sat on a wooden stool in front of a large table. Upon the table was another of the glass balls.

He made another one. But why?

Oh, you know why, Joy. Isn't it obvious? It's as plain as the last falling snowflake of winter settling upon the first of the fresh leaves.

Yes, she did know. But even if by now, she somehow didn't, Ludwig's own thoughts from the past interrupted her.

What a miserable life. Each time I have loved I have lost. The second time more brutally painful than the first. What in the name of all that is good would happen should I fall in love a third time? Better to be rid of it. If joy escapes me then it shall escape all...

He turned the glass ball, and a moment later a shining light whizzed inside it and began sadly swimming around. Ludwig inspected it curiously. It was the memory of a young boy. He was with a woman, his mother most likely. Together they were in a kitchen and rolling out what looked to be dough of some kind.

Oh, tell me it's not gingerbread.

Ludwig clearly thought the same. He turned from the ball and walked into the darkness of his home.

Once more, the being marched forwards. Each step seemed more painful to him than the last, and Joy understood what this thing was. It was Ludwig. Another form of him at least. His future ghost perhaps, for Joy had heard it once told that such spirits were doomed to wander eternally in the wide world to witness the things they might have turned to happiness, only chose not to. Such a sad, sad affair.

And here, Joy felt, was the being's final memory. It couldn't bear to watch now, covering the area where its face should be with handless hands, sobbing weepless tears, sitting in eternal misery.

The glass ball was filled with light from many worlds. People from every planet in the universe swirled around it, their memories forever trapped inside Ludwig's contraption. But he wasn't looking at it. He was busy preparing something else entirely.

They think they can stop me, do they? Let's see what they make of my army of metal men.

Joy hadn't a clue how these things operated, but she watched in horrified awe as he managed to switch several of the machines on. Their eyes lit up dully, and they marched off, rifles in hand, ready to take on the humans who dared to try and stop their master. Each time the humans gained ground, Ludwig would take his machine and move further away from the fighting, always to somewhere cold, dark and concealed. Finally he had climbed the great mountain that had so sleepily watched over the village that Lothar had grown up in.

And Ludwig simply sat in the dark, utterly alone, and waited for every piece of joy to be collected in his miserable machine. It seemed very apt to Joy that his only friends were thoughtless, emotionless, empty men.

~

'Enough!'

Joy blurted the word out aloud before she could help herself. Ludwig and Lothar both stood looking at her, confused. Her face was filled with tears. Ludwig's life was terribly sad. But it had been the child's death that had set her tears flowing so hurriedly down her cheeks.

How awful. How truly, truly awful.

'My lady,' Lothar started. 'What happened to you?'

'It would take too long to explain,' Joy breathed. Her voice was shaking.

'She's from another world,' Ludwig said plainly, eyes fixed on Joy. 'And it looks as though she has an... ability of some sort.'

Lothar looked completely bemused. Ludwig too, seemed interested, but Joy thought that he was almost certainly concerned about what she may now know.

'Your life has been very sad, Ludwig,' she said. 'You would have my sympathy if you hadn't tried to destroy the entire universe because of your own broken heart.'

Ludwig now looked angry, but no fury came from him. He simply scowled at Joy and said nothing.

'Sorry...' Lothar said. He walked a pace towards Joy and shook his head. 'I feel I'm quite lost in this conversation.'

'Yeah...' Joy said. 'You probably are. But I suppose you've worked a lot of it out for yourself. That ball over there – the things that are glowing inside are people's memories of joyful times. That's why everyone's been getting so sad. Their good memories are locked up in there. He's got them all.'

'Well,' Lothar said, looking at the ball. 'Can't we release them?'

That was the moment that Joy's heart fell to the floor. It was as if she'd known all along what she would eventually have to do, but kept that thought locked away in the back of her mind. Now that Lothar had asked her a direct question about it, she had to face it.

'Go ahead,' Ludwig's voice broke the uncomfortable silence. He was looking at Joy with a hint of a smirk on his face. 'Tell him. Tell him what happens if you break the orb.'

Joy looked Lothar in the eye. 'If it's broken, all the memories inside will return to their owners, and joy will be restored.'

A wild look came upon the face of Lothar then. He marched towards the glowing glass ball. 'Well then, what are we waiting for?'

'No! Stop!' Joy raced towards him and placed a hand firmly on his shoulder. His gaze remained fixed on the glass ball, knowing that the end of his years of torment and grief were just a few steps away.

'You'll die!' Joy cried. 'If you break it, you'll *die!*'

He took no notice of this; he pushed against Joy, who now had both of her hands on him, trying to stop his relentless progression towards the ball. There seemed to be no talking him out of this.

'Please, Lothar!' Joy pleaded. 'Whoever destroys it dies! It happened to his daughter!'

Lothar stopped pushing at Joy. His head suddenly snapped to the side and his eyes met Joy's. He looked shocked. His eyes sang a song too sad to be heard aloud. And yet they were also disbelieving, as though what Joy had just said couldn't possibly be true. Then they looked at Ludwig.

'You... lost your child?' Lothar whispered.

Ludwig remained as still as stone. In that moment, Joy thought that the man might have done or said the most horrid of things and yet would still be pitied. Losing a child was an unbearable thought. Enough to drive someone to do the things that Ludwig had done?

Ludwig said nothing, but nodded. It seemed Lothar couldn't bear to look at the man anymore. Instead, he continued to look at the orb, glowing sadly joyous in the dark cave.

'I am sorry,' Lothar said. 'Truly.'

Still, Ludwig said nothing, but his gaze now shifted to where Lothar and Joy's was. For many minutes, none of them spoke. But in that time, Joy's head was spinning with a thousand thoughts.

Crash-landed. Hope gone. Can never return home. Too late for me. Nobody here for me. No friends. No family. Nothing.

'Well...' Lothar's voice piped up. 'Someone has to do *something*...'

He made to move, but Joy stopped him once again.

'Yes,' she said. 'Someone has to break it. Return joy to the world. To all the worlds. But it can't be you, Lothar.'

When he spoke again, Lothar's voice held something inside it that Joy hadn't been prepared for: anger.

'Not *me*? And why not? Why shouldn't I be the one to end this? Years and years I've watched my home being decimated! Sitting there not being able to do a thing about it! Eating food and growing fat while my friends and my family were all out there dying! Well, it's my turn now.'

'No!' Joy insisted. 'No, Lothar, it really *can't* be you!'

Lothar's eyes were filled with rage now. 'Who then? You can't mean that you want to sacrifice *your* life for this? You are too young, girl. You have your entire life to live.'

'I'm not as young as Yunie,' Joy said, calmly, and Lothar's whole aura changed in an instant. 'You're a *father,* Lothar. To a beautiful little girl who's going to think the world of you when she can feel happy. Think of it, Lothar. Don't you want to be there when Yunie feels joy properly for the first time in her life? Don't you want to watch her grow up? Show her the world, and perhaps even worlds beyond yours. Love her, laugh with her, be her *father.* You can't sacrifice all of that, Lothar. But it's already over for me. It was over the moment I came to your world. I have nothing. Nobody. Allow me to break the orb. It will be my honour.'

For a moment, Joy thought that Lothar was considering this. For a brief time, she might have been convinced that he was about to let Joy sacrifice herself for the good of the universe. But she was wrong.

Neither of them said anything more, but each began racing, scrambling, fighting forwards, trying to hold back the other from reaching the orb first. Joy stumbled but caught herself, Lothar clutched at her, trying to hold her back. But it was useless in the end; something within her had awoken. She couldn't be stopped.

Even as she reached the ball, Lothar still clutched at Joy's waist, but it was futile. By the time she heard the glass break, she'd slipped completely out of his grasp. She collapsed to the cold stone floor and had a brief moment to be filled with the deepest awe as the cave filled with majestic light before she closed her eyes. Her last thought before slipping away was of Hope. She saw her somewhere a billion light years

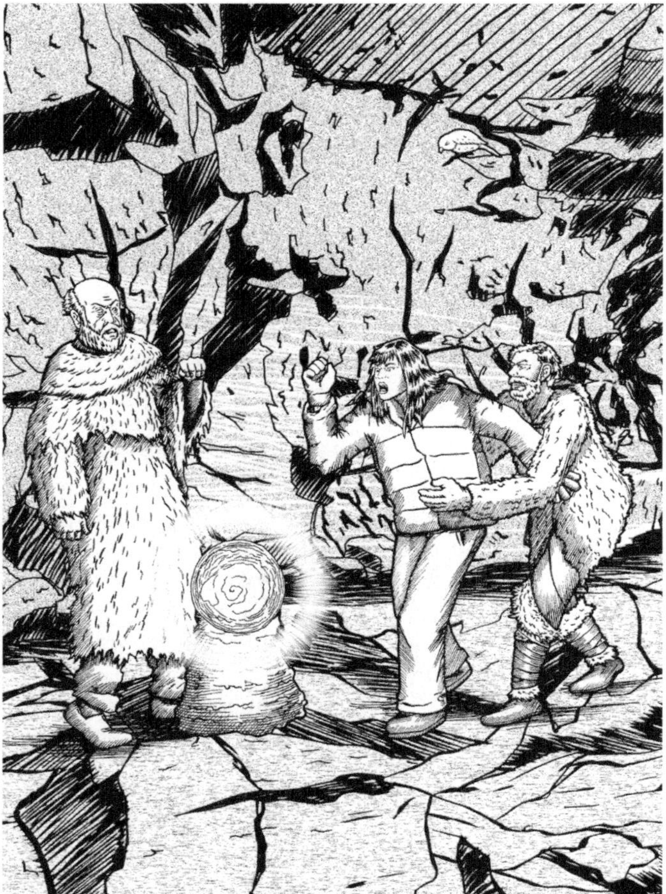

away in some other universe. She was with Yunie and Ludwig's own daughter. Together they laughed heartily for the end of war and the return of happiness as they rolled out dough for making gingerbread.

***

The golden light completely surrounded the frozen planet, and if anyone had been looking, they might have mistaken the place for a world full of beaches, not snow and ice. Indeed, it looked more like a star than a planet now as memories were returned, spirits were awoken, and joy found its glorious path back to where it truly belonged: in the hearts and minds of all.

Folk who had become withdrawn and accustomed to hiding in their bedrooms suddenly smiled, flung open their doors and searched frantically for their neighbours. Children's eyes lit up and their hearts began drumming against their chests with this strange and wild new sensation. Singing filled the air and dancing lined the streets. Joy was returned at last.

And it didn't stop on this planet. Ludwig's broken machine released its light all around the previously darkening universe; into every corner of it. Tears were shed, hugs were shared, songs were sung in countless languages. All was finally well.

Almost well.

For even within the hearts of those furthest away from the source of all their misery and now their glee, it was somehow felt, somehow known that this victory must have come with a price to someone.

And what a price it was.

***

'Joy! Joy! Oh, my young lady, you must wake!'

She blinked. The cave was dark again. Lothar crouched over her, a look of concern on his tired face.

'I'm…' Joy started. 'I'm alive?'

Lothar smiled then, and it lifted Joy's spirits more than she thought anything in her entire life had.

'Of course you're alive!' Lothar said. 'Come with me. I think Ludwig should not be alone.'

'Ludwig?' Joy questioned, but there was no time to dwell on it. Lothar lifted Joy to her feet and together they made for the tunnel that they had arrived through earlier.

'Take care,' Lothar said. He indicated towards the place the orb had been sitting. It had indeed been shattered. Shards of broken glass lay on the rocky floor. Joy accidentally crunched a few small pieces on her way out of the cave. As she followed Lothar, she felt a warm, familiar pat on her shoulder and knew that her friend had joined her once again.

'Hello, Fortune,' Joy said. 'Where were you after your song?'

'A clever bobin indeed, that one,' Lothar said. 'Reminds me of a toy I once had.'

'Yeah,' Joy said. 'I suppose that one didn't sing though.'

'Only in my dreams,' Lothar said, and although Joy couldn't see it, she knew a smile accompanied this remark. 'Come now, we're running out of time.'

***

Outside, dawn had finally arrived. For a moment, it looked as though the glorious light from earlier had reappeared, bathing the mountainside in beautiful light. Now that she could see this place properly, she rejoiced to see how striking a land it was. Snow covered the ground everywhere Joy could see, and in the distance was a vast mountain range. Far below she could just make out Lothar's village, and could even swear that she saw a flicker of light come from it. Life was returning.

'There,' Lothar's voiced interrupted. He indicated towards an open piece of ground beside the rising sun. Ludwig lay there, his chest gently rising and falling. Lothar turned to face Joy. 'Let's go to him.'

'I'll go,' Joy said. 'Why don't you head back to the cabin and find Yunie? I imagine the first meeting of father and daughter in these new, happier times would be better done in private. I'll join you later.'

Lothar considered this for a brief moment before nodding. 'Thank you, my friend. I'll see you soon.'

With that, Lothar walked away, and Joy went to Ludwig.

He looked at her as she arrived. His face was pained. In his right hand he clutched a rock. The hand and the rock were covered in blood.

'You... *you* broke the orb?' Joy asked, unbelievingly.

Ludwig smiled for a moment and then nodded.

'Why?' Joy asked.

'I...' Ludwig started. His next words came slowly and quietly. 'I didn't think there was any good in this world. I never would have imagined a single person should want to make a sacrifice for the good of others. But then I saw that there were at least two who would.'

Joy knelt beside the old man now. He was shivering. Just as she had with Eric the night previously, she held his hand. Fortune fluttered to a rock beside Ludwig, and again watched with her innocently curious look that had become so familiar to Joy.

'I've done a terrible thing. Terrible,' Ludwig continued. 'I was selfish. It was right that I should have grieved for my daughter, but it was wrong of me to force my grief on everyone else. I have paid.'

Joy allowed a tear to fall from her cheek. 'I'm so very sorry about your daughter. You loved her, didn't you?'

Ludwig smiled again, as though he had somehow forgotten his deep bereavement and sat now with his daughter, playing games and laughing with her. Joy's heart sank into an ocean of compassionate sorrow.

'Yes,' Ludwig said. 'Yes, I did. And I'm thankful for it. I'm going to see her now, you know.'

And then Joy had to ask a question that even her own Sense had not been able to answer.

'What was her name? Your daughter?'

Ludwig's gaze now fixed on the last star in the morning sky as it faded from sight. As his eyes shut for their final time, he whispered his child's name to Joy:

'Mercy.'

And the old man said no more.

***

Yunie was delighted to see Joy. Outside the cabin, the child flung her arms around her. Her father, while wiping at his face, stood back and laughed heartily.

'Joy! Oh, thank you for finding my father! And thank you for looking after me! And I'm sorry I didn't talk much! I'm so happy to see you! You said you'd come back and you did, you did, *you did!*'

'Yeah,' Joy said, squeezing Yunie close to her. 'Of course I did! And didn't I say your father would too?'

Snow began to fall once more, and the three of them headed back inside the cabin to wait for it to calm a little before they began their descent down the great mountain. Having mostly stayed up all night, they were all exhausted, and it was decided that they should all rest before their climb down. Lothar got into the bed with Yunie, and Joy laid down some soft material on the wooden floor where she managed to make herself comfortable. Fortune had joined them inside and had already rested her beak into her feathery back on the mantelpiece above the fire. At first it was useless for Joy to try to sleep; an endless array of thoughts swirled around inside her mind, but she was eventually lulled to sleep by the gentle tapping of snowdrops on the roof and window of the cabin.

Later, they were all awakened by a joyous sound.

'Is that... *singing?*' Yunie's little voice piped up.

Joy lifted her head from the floor, and heard it too. The very same song she had heard sung by the ghosts of the past, floating up from the village below.

> *Gaudete, gaudete Christus est natus*
> *Ex maria virgine, gaudete*

But this time it *did* sound happy. It sounded as gleeful as anything Joy had heard in all of her life.

'It's stopped snowing,' Lothar remarked. He was only partly right; the snowfall had simply lessened in force. But his meaning was clear to Joy: it was time to descend.

***

The journey down had not taken very long. Even little Yunie was able to make good progress, even moving more swiftly than her father at times. The village was in plain view the entire time, and they saw with elation that first one light and then another and another had been lit. Lothar pointed out with enthusiasm that many of them were different colours. The old Christmas lanterns had been lit.

'How do they make them all different colours, Father?' Yunie asked. 'It's beautiful!'

Lothar laughed and gently wrapped an arm around his daughter. 'Do you know, my daughter, there was once a time I knew the answer to that, and now I've quite forgotten.'

'Different types of metal, probably,' Joy said.

Lothar looked at her, puzzled. 'That's it, I think. How would you know?'

And now it was Joy's turn to laugh. In all the adventure of the night, all the excitement of the return of happiness, she'd completely forgotten that she was almost a total stranger to Lothar, and that he knew nothing of her special ability.

'I'll tell you the full story later,' she smiled. 'Let's just get you and Yunie home!'

She was interrupted by a sudden blast from some music just ahead of them. From within some trees not far off, a quartet of musicians playing instruments which looked and sounded to Joy very much like the trumpets from her own planet. They rang out triumphantly, playing a tune that sounded like one of their Christmas carols. As they played, they marched towards Joy, Lothar and Yunie. A man Joy didn't recognise from any of Lothar's memories strode forwards, a look of glee and yet also wonder on his face. He was around the same age as Lothar, his hair had just begun to grey and Joy could see the years of lines his face had accumulated begin to almost vanish upon seeing Lothar.

'Lothar!' he cried. 'My dearest Lothar! Is it really you?'

'Mikkel!' Lothar said. His voice was filled with the same wondrous pleasure that had been on the man's face.

The two embraced as the trumpeters rang out their final chord, and then watched the pair with smiles on their faces. When they finally let go of each other, Lothar turned to Joy and Yunie, introduced Yunie with pride and Joy with happiness. Lothar had last seen Mikkel some years before Yunie was born. He was called to the war and then sadness overcame him. He hid in a dark cave for many weeks and months, almost succumbing completely to his grief before he was finally freed by the breaking of Ludwig's orb. The gathered folk had many questions for Lothar and Joy: *what happened? Did it really have something to do with you, Lothar? When did little Yunie get so tall? Where in the wide world did Joy come from? Why did we all feel so glum in the first place?*

They talked merrily on their way back to the village. Lothar, it seemed, couldn't help but laugh wholeheartedly at what anyone said. When the village was close, Joy could see that it was indeed lit up in colours of all description; the sun was beginning to set again and she could hear music from the village, could smell wonderful food cooking, could feel warmness and happiness envelop her. Yunie had taken her hand and the pair of them walked behind Lothar, Mikkel and the musicians as their pace quickened, keen to arrive at the village. She closed her eyes and drew a deep breath in from her nose. She felt as though she could live in this moment forever. She'd never felt so happy.

And yet…

And yet something still wasn't right. She'd done it; she'd completed her impossible mission to restore joy to the universe. She'd helped save Lothar and Yunie. The old village was full of life once more.

And she wondered how Hope felt now. What she was doing. Where she was. Was she even thinking of her big sister?

And then she knew. She knew that however happy she might feel in all her life, always there would be this lingering sadness within her. And that was the price of it. Her sacrifice for the good of the universe. She looked up to the first of the night stars, and finding the one that her Sense told her shone down upon her sister, she hoped and wished that she knew there was no other way. The price of joy was not a breaking but a wounding of a heart that would never truly heal.

***

They were greeted in the village by a celebration the magnitude of which none of them had ever seen before. Songs were sung, food was eaten, beer, wine and whisky were drunk. The village was alive with laughter, stories, music and total, wholesome joy.

Lothar had told his whole story to Mikkel, with Joy filling in the parts she could that Lothar hadn't known. One of the musicians had been busy scribbling everything they said onto a large piece of parchment. This was a story that should never be forgotten.

Of course, there was sadness too; the great graveyard loomed in the distance and was as full of brave men and women as it had been before the return of joy. Ludwig's orb could not change the past, but the people who fought hard against the great grief would never be forgotten. Indeed, there was speak in the village that night of marking a day each year in remembrance of these bravest of people, for bravest among the brave they were. Who could fight against their own grief, especially when things looked impossibly stacked against them? It certainly had taken special people to do just that, and although they had fallen without realising their goal, they would be remembered for all time simply because they tried. For trying is all anyone can ask of any person.

Joy was offered many strange foods she'd never had before. Most were apologetic at the lack of anything very substantial; nobody had been to hunt or gather foods of any kind since the sadness had taken them. There were plenty of sweet berries however (Fortune enjoyed these), some bread and pastries, tea made from what the people called "snow herbs", and the shavings from the bark of a special kind of tree that grew locally. These were boiled and then cooled, and when they were eaten, they tasted to Joy like chocolate.

Many people were eager to talk to Joy. She must have met every person in the village that night. At one point, she had several of them gathered around a small fire where she told them of Gylfandell, of her planet as a whole, and of her journey to their planet, and her mission to find out how to restore happiness. She was tired, but she tried her best to describe things such as planets and spacecrafts, concepts which were completely alien to these people. She wondered at first if they thought her mad, but was reassured when a lady spoke after she told of her crash-landing on the planet.

'So *that's* what that strange thing to the south was! We found your ship, Miss. Buried in the snow, just the way you said it was. It was as cold as death itself.'

Eventually, Joy was overcome with fatigue, and Lothar took her into his home where he made up a bed for her in one of the rooms of his house that had been empty for these last few years.

***

It was strange to wake in a place she'd mainly only seen in someone else's memories. Joy had awoken early and spent much of the morning looking out of the window where the snow was dropping gently, and the sleepy village slowly awoke and came alive with folk clearing the paths in front of each other's homes. She smiled widely when she saw that Lothar and Yunie had both woken even earlier than she had, and were hard at work ploughing the snow away from paths. She threw on her boots and coat and ran down to join them.

'Joy! You're awake!'

Yunie was the first to spot her. She ran to her and once again wrapped her little arms ardently around her waist.

Joy joined in with the work, as did nearly every person in the village. Folk were scattered around everywhere clearing snow, digging out buried houses, hanging more decorations and travelling outside of the village to gather as much food and resources as possible; much had been pulled together for the previous night's celebration, but most of it had been expended.

That first day in the village was a tiresome but happy one. By the end of the day, the village looked almost as it once had in Lothar's youth. Comparing those times to now, Joy knew that the village still seemed somewhat bare; many of the houses, though dug out of the snow and recovered, lay empty. Some who had gone out to war, or had vanished from the village some years before, hadn't returned. And of course, many had, but were now to be found under the ground in the same place Lothar used to sledge as a boy.

Fortune visited Joy plenty of times, even when more bobins began fluttering around and singing their beautiful songs. Sometimes at night, Joy could swear she heard some of them sing the first few notes of *Silent Night,* but they would trail off and the tune would be lost.

Are they learning it? Is Fortune teaching them it?

And most of the times she would hear it, Joy would nod off into a pleasant sleep.

Not long after, happiness burst into the village like nothing Joy had ever experienced before.

It was around midday. The sun was brightly shining through the opening in the clouds, but it was cold, as always. Joy had taken a walk with Yunie, and the pair had engaged in a snowball fight, laughing heartily as they flung their missiles at one another. Their fun was interrupted by a call.

'Hello! You there!'

Joy turned and saw a group of people. An elderly man and woman, joined by two others: a younger man and woman. The old man held a walking stick, and was being aided by the younger woman, who had a small but deep scar on her left cheek.

'Hello!' Joy called as brightly as she could. 'Are you the next of the returners to this village?'

'We are,' said the younger man. They approached Joy and Yunie now, and the child looked up at these people with a glowing intrigue.

'I don't know your face,' the old man said.

'No,' Joy said. 'I come from a place a long way from here. My name is Joy.'

At that, the four strangers laughed.

'Joy, indeed!' the younger woman said. 'It's been many years since last I was home. And I come back to find Joy staring me in the face!'

'Tell me,' the older woman said. 'Is there a man in this village by the name of Lothar?'

Joy felt a chill run down her body. She recognised these people now. They were all older, yes, but their faces remained much the same as the ones she'd known from Lothar's memories.

But the old man... It couldn't be...

'Yunie,' Joy breathed. 'Run along and fetch your father. Tell him to come quickly. Go!'

Without asking any questions, Yunie ran as fast as she could towards her house.

'Y... Yunie?' the younger woman gasped. 'You said her name was Yunie? And she's to fetch her father?'

And Joy couldn't stop the tears coming. She wanted to speak with these people so desperately, had what seemed to be a thousand questions. But she couldn't. She just stood there in shock and happiness and grief and awe.

Yunie ran back with her father a moment later. Lothar stood and looked at his family with his mouth wide open.

'Jonas? Annika? Mother?'

And standing now completely with his walking stick alone, Sander, who, it seemed, did **not** die, strode forwards.

'My son...'

Joy felt her old bobin friend land softly on her shoulder. It would appear that even Fortune did not want to miss this scene unfold.

Lothar looked at Sander with disbelieving eyes. *'Father?* But... how?'

But his question would have to wait, for the old man could bear to be parted from his son no longer. He dropped his walking stick into the snow and ran to his son, clutching him tightly and weeping to see him.

Then Yunie's voice piped up. 'Father? These are... your family?'

Malin looked at the child with watered and doting eyes. 'His family and *yours*, my dear. I did not expect to find a grandchild here!'

Joy saw that love swelled and filled the hearts of each family member. She watched from the sides with her feathered friend as the family openly wept tears of happiness. She wasn't standing alone for long; it was Annika who first asked Lothar about Joy, and Lothar told his sister with enthusiasm of how this mysterious young woman had come from afar to bring glee back into the world.

'Not just the world. The universe!' Yunie corrected.

'The... universe?' Jonas asked, confusedly.

'Let's go home and exchange stories,' Lothar said. 'I do believe all of us have much to share!'

They ate and drank as they talked, and it was a busy day as news of the reappearance of Lothar's family spread quickly around the village, and they had to welcome many guests to their home. Each of them brought gifts with them, and it was just like the Christmas of old.

'I am sorry!' Malin said to each guest. 'We have nothing to give in return! We shall endeavour to give twice as much to each of you this Christmas!'

But nobody found any offence in this. They were all happy to see them, and particularly to hear of Sander's tale. A friend of his had seen him shot by one of Ludwig's machines, and had presumed he was dead. The man who now lay in the grave marked with

Sanders' name was really called Fredrik; he had had no friends or family left, and none who could properly identify him. Sander had somehow been mixed up with him.

'A sad tale indeed,' Mikkel had remarked upon hearing it. 'Poor Fredrik died and nobody mourned him. Worse, there were those who mistakenly mourned the wrong man.'

'I remember him well,' Sander said. 'I shall see to it that the headstone is changed and some appropriate words are etched onto it to remember him by.'

They talked late into the night, eating and drinking, laughing and weeping. And still, there was that horrid place in Joy's heart that couldn't allow for true happiness. It was Annika who noticed the glum look on Joy's face first.

'Joy, my friend,' she said. 'Why do you look so unhappy?'

Joy simply stared into the crackling fireplace. Outside, the first snowflakes of another flurry began., and a bright, faraway star shone enough light that it was reflected in Joy's tearful eye.

'My sister,' Joy said. 'Hope. I just wonder what she's doing now. I wonder how much she'll remember me. I wonder if she's truly happy.'

And then Joy allowed herself to openly weep at the table.

'Oh, how I wish I could see her again!'

That was when the table began to shake. The plates and knives and forks rattled. From outside, a distant, familiar hum sounded.

Joy snapped her head up at once. 'It... it can't be!'

Saying nothing more she flung on her coat and darted outside, Lothar's family joining her. Outside, every villager had leapt out of their house to see what in the world was happening. Looking upwards, Joy saw a magnificent sight. A spacecraft, larger than the one she had stolen. An official looking one. All the way from Gylfandell.

'Joy!' Yunie called from over the noise. 'Are these *your* people?'

Joy didn't allow herself to feel happy or hopeful in that moment. Not yet. Not as the ship landed behind the village a little, on top of the same hill Joy had stood with Fortune when she first set eyes on the place. Not as she, and the rest of the village ran up the hill, panting as they went. Not when the side door of the craft hissed and then slowly opened.

Only when three people stepped out. Her sister, and their lost mother and father.

'*Joy!!*' Hope darted out of the craft and hugged her weeping big sister.

'I knew you'd do it, Joy! You did, didn't you? You found a way! You brought happiness back! And Mum and Dad came back to find us! Only you were gone and I didn't know if we could get you! But Dad made them come! He made them come to get you! Oh, Joy! Joy!'

For the next week, introductions were made, songs were sung, food was shared and more people came back to the village. Hope and her mother and father had come with representatives of the observation department, who were full of good cheer and promised Joy that she would not face any consequences for the stolen spacecraft. The situation was deemed an exceptional circumstance, and word had it that all of Gylfandell was filled with a joy never before seen, and were anxious to greet the young woman who had returned it to them.

'You won't recognise the place!' Joy's mother said. 'I can't wait to show you!'

On the eighth day, Lothar's heart soared as Yunie's mother, Freyja returned. She flung Yunie up in the air and caught her upon seeing her, and Joy thought that things now could not be any better. She wanted to stay here on the frozen planet for much longer, but she knew that the representatives from her workplace also had families, and that they should be with them in this joyous time.

On the last day, the whole village gathered to watch Joy depart. Joy promised them that she would be back.

'Perhaps at Christmas time,' Joy said. 'Although it always seems like Christmas here, nowadays.'

'Christmas...' Joy's father mused. 'Perhaps this is something we can take back to our planet.'

'I like that idea,' Hope said.

'Me too,' Yunie agreed.

Joy took her time embracing each of her newest and dearest of friends. Her last, longest and deepest of which was for Lothar, a man she had shared so much with, and a man who understood better than any the importance of what they had done.

When all goodbyes were said, and all tears were shed, Joy went with her family into the spacecraft. The villagers watched in wonder as it rose impressively into the air and vanished out of sight towards the brightest star in the sky.

And so it was that Joy and Hope set out together into the wide universe. And with them, it is said, went Fortune.

Acknowledgements

My heartfelt thanks once again goes to my friend Jenny Konsen for reading this book, providing invaluable feedback and spotting mistakes. This book would not be as good without your help.

Thank you to MVMET, the brilliantly talented artist who produced the original hand-drawn images found within the pages of this book. It was a real pleasure and privilege to work with you and I wish you a universe of success in the future.

Thank you so very much to my daughter, Mirryn, who is at the heart of my inspiration for most things I write, and who named a character in this story – Hunter the great wolf, who later became known as Woe. I said once before that you are the light by which I can navigate my way through life, and it holds truer every day.

And a hearty thank you to you, the reader, who gave this story a shot. I very much hope you enjoyed reading it.

It means the world (and worlds beyond).

If you enjoyed this book, please consider leaving a review on Amazon or Goodreads. This will help me reach more readers!

Follow me on social media for all the latest.

Sign up to my mailing list at www.chrisamorris.com

Printed in Great Britain
by Amazon